THE CHANGE

GUY ADAMS

SOLARIS

Available: UK / July 2017 / ISBN 9781781085813 • US / TBD
For press enquiries please contact Rob Power on +44 (0)1865 792 201 (ext: 246)
or rob.power@rebellion.co.uk

First published 2017 by Solaris
an imprint of Rebellion Publishing Ltd,
Riverside House, Osney Mead,
Oxford, OX2 0ES, UK

www.solarisbooks.com

ISBN: 978 1 78108 581 3

A CIP catalogue record for this book is available
from the British Library.

Designed & typeset by Rebellion Publishing

Printed in the UK

1

LONDON
ORBITAL

Chapter One

HE WOKE TO the smell of petrol and smoke. It wasn't the pleasant wood smoke of barbecues and winter fires, it was acidic; black curls of burning plastic and rubber. Chemical smoke. It burned the back of his throat, like trying to breathe static.

Sitting up, he brushed dust from the chest of his coat. His face felt wet. He touched his cheek and found blood. This didn't seem surprising, though he was in no pain and had no memory of how it had happened. Perhaps it was the *idea* of wounds that he was used to, like someone who has had a lot of them.

He got to his feet, his legs aching because he'd been lying on them, trapped nerves and the bristle of pins and needles.

The road was full of abandoned cars. Some were intact, others had blossomed into roadside flowers: petals of gouged metal and a dew frosting of shattered glass. They were nose-to to-bumper on all four lanes, stretching as far as he could see.

To his right there was a city. The shape of it was familiar. Even though he knew very little at that moment, he still knew London.

He bent down to look at his reflection in a wing-mirror. The blood was running from a small cut on his forehead, trickling down his face and washing the dust away *en route*. It gave his reflection interest, there was no other reason to look at it—it wasn't a face he knew.

He walked off the road, looking for somewhere to sit in the long grass of the embankment. Somewhere to get his head straight.

Every few seconds there was the distant roar of engines, like monsters fighting one another just over the horizon. Sometimes the breeze carried the sound of shouting and laughter. Sooner or later the people making that noise were bound to head in his direction. He wasn't sure how he felt about that.

He found water, a small amount collected in the rusty bowl of a stray hubcap. He dipped his fingers, meaning to clean his face, the water stung his skin and he was thankful he hadn't tried to drink it.

He was hot. He made to pull off the long leather coat he was wearing before deciding to check the pockets first. His fingers pulled out a small, black notebook but as he could neither eat nor drink it he dropped it to the ground and carried on searching. There was half a packet of chewing gum—the sort that came in a foil-sealed tray, like pills—nothing else. He took off the coat, sat down and popped a piece of the gum into his mouth. It was strong menthol and made the inside of his mouth cold.

He picked up the notebook. It was old, battered and creased. He held it up to his nose and sniffed: leather. It occurred to him how ridiculous it was to know the smell of leather but not be able to recall your own name. A strap of elastic was threaded through the back cover then wrapped around the front to hold its pages shut. He snapped the elastic back and opened it up.

This book belongs to: Howard Philips

announced the front page. Surrounding the text were various sketches and doodles, from vague swirls to people's faces. He turned the page.

The Change—Notes on the New World

It didn't sound very interesting. If the notebook was his—and he had no reason to doubt it—the news was not good: not only was he called "Howard", but he also wrote boring books. He read on, in the hope that things improved:

> I wasn't there for The Change, if I had been I would be dead. Nobody who saw The Change survived, that's why there aren't many people left.

I met a man once who SAID he'd seen The Change, said he'd seen 'the Gods' appear and begin to change stuff. But then he also used to wear dead cats on his head. He was crazy and nobody believes crazy people, not even now when there are so many of them.

It happened on the morning of the 6th of January. People call them 'Gods', the creatures that appeared. They call them that not because anyone would pray to them or build a church for them, they call them that because it's the biggest word for a thing people know.

Howard looked up from the book at the sound of an explosion from somewhere in the distance. He looked along the road but could see nothing.

He felt uncomfortable out in the open. It would be better to get moving.

There was the sound of engines again, high and grating like giant mosquitoes. He put the notebook back into his coat pocket, slung the coat over his shoulder and walked onto the road.

He wondered where all the cars had been going before there got to be so many they couldn't go anywhere. Some people had abandoned them—presumably trying to escape whatever had driven them away on foot—but many still had occupants. Howard looked in one. On the back seat, bones were woven into one another, perhaps the rotted remnant of a hugging couple. The bone was dressed with thin flags of skin, dried sharp and tough like pet treats. The skeleton of the driver had a splintered forehead and the grey plastic of the dashboard was spattered with black gunk from which thick moss grew. Whether he had smashed his own brains out or not was impossible to tell.

Howard didn't look in any more cars.

He saw a thin German Shepherd sunning itself on the hard shoulder. Its ribs protruded as far as its tongue. If it weren't for the faint sound of panting and the tremble of breath in its belly, Howard would have thought it dead. He walked cautiously past it, expecting it to attack. Perhaps it was too weak. It growled but didn't move, just watched him with bloodshot eyes.

It wasn't the only sign of life. Rats scurried between the cars, hugging the darkness beneath their chassis, fearful of the crows and ravens that circled overhead.

One fat bird stared at Howard as he walked past. He stopped to stare back. It was perched on the roof of a car, head tilted to watch him sideways-on. Its perfect black circle of an eye gave no clue to its thoughts. He crouched down, picked up a stone and hurled it at the bird. The shot was wide, but the bird took off anyway.

Howard met his first human being half an hour later.

His hair and beard were so long that Howard was uncertain whether the man was wearing anything else. He was cooking a raven—perhaps the same one he had seen earlier—on a spit. Its eyes wept milky tears into the flames where they hissed to steam.

The man waved him over.

Howard pulled his coat on—easier to run if the man turned out to be dangerous—and walked over to the small fire.

The man gave him a smile with less teeth than sincerity. 'You're not one of *them*,' he said, gesturing vaguely in the direction Howard had come from. It was a statement rather than a question and needed no answer, which was good as Howard had no idea whether he *was* 'one of them' or not. 'No oil,' the man continued, 'they always have oil,' he waved his hand over his face, 'like Indian war paint.'

The man wasn't as old as Howard had assumed by his hair and beard, maybe only in his thirties, but his voice was strange, foreign. 'I do not like *them*,' the man said, 'they are too much with their *clang, boom, steam...*' He turned the raven on its spit, a high-pitched whine emanating from its belly as gasses escaped in the heat. 'I do not believe we should draw attention to ourselves, not anymore... stay quiet, stay safe...' He pointed to the ground next to him. 'Sit down, I kill only black birds, you are too big for my fire.'

Howard sat down.

'You eat?' the man asked.

'Please, If you can spare it.' Howard replied, 'I haven't

eaten for…' He realised he had no idea how long it had been.

The man nodded. 'We will share.' He lifted the bird from the flames and reached behind him for a knife. 'You should not eat with a person whose name you do not know,' he said as he held the point of the spit against the ground and began to cut. 'My name's Teodor.'

'Howard.'

The man passed him a wedge of crisp meat. 'Eat then, Howard.'

So he did.

After their meal, the man showed no interest in talking. He simply lay back in the grass of the hard shoulder and closed his eyes. Howard watched the man start to doze, pulled the notebook out of his pocket and flicked to where he had stopped reading.

So… how do we even know the little bit we do? From those who saw the events second-hand, through photographs or video footage. This was enough to send them mad, but not enough to kill them. As I said before, the world now has a LOT of crazy people in it. Some THINGS appeared in the skies (and the water, I have heard lots of stories of monsters in the sea). They changed our world. Nobody knows HOW. Nobody knows WHY. Nobody cares either, it's the least of our worries. Waking up one morning to find the streets filled with dead people and lunatics was bad, what followed was WORSE.

There are monsters now. Impossible things everywhere you look. Everything we used to take for granted as either 'real' or 'fantasy' has changed. ANYTHING can be out there now, anything at all...

Howard closed the book, it wasn't helping to have his own voice—assuming it *was* him that had written those words—tell him how hopeless everything was.

Teodor was snoring loudly. Flies buzzed around the forest of his beard looking for bits of meat in its branches. The sun was getting low in the sky and the sound of distant motors was building in the distance. He felt twitchy. He had been sat still too long.

He got to his feet, meaning to sneak away. Teodor was a light sleeper though.

'You do not travel at night,' he said, opening one eye to look at Howard. 'The night-time is about danger. Find somewhere dark and safe, the back of a car, *whatever*... but get off the road and *stay* off it until dawn.'

'Thank you.' Howard felt guilty sneaking off, but Teodor didn't seem concerned. He closed his one eye and fell silent again.

Howard walked quickly between the cars. He was relieved to notice the sound of engines getting quieter. Whoever it was ('with their *clang. boom, steam...*') they didn't seem to be heading in his direction.

As the light faded he chose a small, white van as a good place to rest. He opened the back and checked it was completely empty (he didn't want to wake up with a rat gnawing his cheek). Looking around, making sure nobody was in sight, he climbed in and closed the door behind him. He doubted he would sleep but put his coat on the floor and tried to get comfortable.

He did sleep.

The next thing he knew, he was in complete darkness and surrounded by the roar of motorbike engines. There was laughter and shouting, and Howard pictured mad faces in the shine of headlights, howling at the terrifying things this new world had shown them. He covered himself with his coat, hoping to hide from anyone curious enough to shine a light through the rear windows. Nobody did and eventually the riders moved on.

He woke again later, but this time it wasn't motorbike engines that had disturbed him. Something was moving outside the van. He could hear a vehicle: not as loud as the bikes but the definite hiss and thump of moving motor parts, the faint grinding of metal, of cogs and gears. There was a wet sound too, just underneath the mechanical bump and grind, like wet meat slapping together.

Howard lay as still as he could, even though there was a cramp in his calf from his awkward position. 'The night-time is dangerous,' Teodor had said. Perhaps whatever stood outside was why.

Eventually it moved off and Howard stretched his legs, careful not to shake the van with the movement. He tried to find a more comfortable position and, after a while, returned to sleep.

The morning fell through the windows of the van and he woke with an ache in his back. He shuffled to the back doors, lifted the lock and catch and stepped out onto the road. Stretching, he felt tendons pop back into place all along his spine.

He turned around and saw a thick, red rope that had fallen between the doors. It was Teodor's beard, slick with blood. The man's dead eyes looked down on him from a nest of matted hair.

The rest of the body was nowhere in sight.

Chapter Two

HE RAN, HIS head empty of everything except the urge to keep moving.

The cars stretched on, all different colours and sizes; expensive cars, cheap cars… Who knew there were so many cars?

Short of breath, he stopped running and leaned forward, hands on his knees. His stomach churned and he knew he was going to be sick. He went to the side of the road and threw up into the thick grass alongside the hard shoulder. His eyes watered as his stomach emptied, convulsing repeatedly until there was nothing left to heave. He dropped down to his knees, trying to catch a breath, rubbed at his eyes and spat the foul taste from his mouth.

Behind him there was the rustle of wings. He thought of the raven he had eaten, and shivered.

He got to his feet and turned to see not a raven but a pigeon, pacing on the roof of the car closest to him. It's fat throat wobbled as it cooed. Howard watched it march up and down the roof, it's gnarled talons clicking on the metal.

The cooing grew louder and, looking beyond the pigeon in front of him, he began to see more and more on the cars around him. They were on the roofs and bonnets or perching on the wing mirrors. Hundreds of them, all fixing him with their little black eyes.

Suddenly, they took to the air. The sound of hundreds of wings beating at the same time was like the cracking of a whip. Howard's nerve broke and he turned and ran.

The first wave, maybe fifty birds, curled past him before turning back. He held his hands in front of his face as they flew straight at him. Their beaks tore at the backs of his hands and yanked at his hair. Then they were gone, circling back up into the sky.

For a second, Howard just stood there, feeling the heat of his own wounds as the blood began to flow along his wrists and into the sleeves of his shirt. He could hear the birds circling above him, preparing to attack again.

The second wave came from the rear and sent him rolling between the cars. He pulled himself under the closest, a red Volvo that looked like it could withstand most things life might throw at it. It had survived an apocalyptic event, after all, what were a few homicidal pigeons compared to that?

The flock landed above him. There was the ruffle of feathers and the low warble of countless quivering throats. A few birds dropped to the ground, peering under the car at him. One of them cocked its head to one side and stared, almost comically confused, at him.

There was something unusual about it, something he couldn't quite put his finger on. Its eyes were perhaps a little too large. They were fat and black and looked ready to burst. Its beak was particularly jagged, like the blade of a bread knife, but Howard guessed that was only natural if you pecked at people and cars. It's feathers were ruffled and untidy but, again, that wasn't what made it look wrong, there was something else, something he couldn't quite... *there!*... something was moving beneath the plumage... beneath the *skin*. The thin tail of a black worm poked from it's open mouth before being sucked back in like a strand of spaghetti.

It walked under the car and pecked at his hand. He smacked it as hard as he could. The bird flapped its wings in anger, bouncing between the ground and the underside of the car before making it back into the open air and flying away. It's fear didn't spread to the others. One by one they hopped under the car with him. He could feel their beaks pecking at his ankles, his thighs, working their way up. The few that found their way to his bleeding hands began to pull at the strands of loose skin. This was no good, he needed proper cover, he needed to be inside a car not *under* one. Which meant he needed to risk going back out in the open.

A pigeon crept close again, pecking at his hand. With a growl he grabbed at it and was so surprised to feel his fingers sink into its gelatinous belly that he nearly let go of it. It tilted its head back and screeched. Thrashing black tendrils burst from its mouth and whipped at the air. Howard flung it away, satisfied to hear a dull *crump* as it collided with the hubcap of a nearby car. He didn't know what to make of them. It was as if another creature entirely was wearing the bird as a disguise. This was not a good world to wake up in.

He windmilled his arms and legs, lashing out at the creatures to buy some room, then slid into the open, rolling to his feet. The beating of wings was almost instantly behind him but he had to hope that they would want to attack him in a wide arc, gathering momentum with which to add strength to their beaks and talons. That momentum would take time to build.

He scanned the row of cars ahead of him as he ran, trying to decide which looked the strongest. So many had broken windows, doors hanging off. He needed something intact, something *strong*. The wings grew louder.

He could see the car he wanted, a people carrier that looked more intact than most. He fixed a stare on the black handle of the rear door as the birds pushed the wind before them, ruffling his hair. Closer, closer, closer... He dropped to a skid, his boots kicking up a cloud of dust as the birds shot past him. They turned in the air. Some were too slow, he heard them punch into the cars on either side, a sound like hail on a tin roof as their beaks punctured metal. He jumped to his feet and grabbed at the door handle. It was locked. With a shout of desperation he tried the driver's door, no good. He peered through the dirty glass at the shadows of bodies inside and began to kick at the door in anger. The pigeon-things swooped towards him and he dropped to his haunches, arms over his head, screwing his eyes shut as they came at him.

Suddenly there was a rising and falling wail like an air-raid siren. After a moment, Howard realised the birds weren't touching him. The flapping wings were moving away, not closer. He opened his eyes to see the flock pushing skywards. On the roof of a nearby car, a boy about Howard's age was swinging a strange contraption made from a car exhaust and a length of chain. He wore combat trousers and a baggy suit jacket pulled over a bare chest that was wrapped in an assortment of belts and straps. His face looked tattooed at first glance, like the black swirls that New Zealand Maoris wore. Remembering what poor Teodor had told him Howard realised it was probably engine oil ('they' wore it 'like Indian war paint' he had said). The boy stopped swinging the exhaust pipe and the noise stopped. He walked down from the roof of the car, his heavy boots popping and bending the metal of the car bonnet as he stamped across it.

'You *so* don't know your Highway Code,' the boy said. 'Rule Number One: don't feed the pigeons.'

Chapter Three

THE BOY WAS probably mad, but Howard wasn't going to hold it against him, he was sure it took a little insanity just to survive these days.

'The pigeons,' he said, taking the time to look at the wounds on his hands now that he was safe, 'there was something weird about them.'

'There's something weird about most animals now,' the boy replied. 'I've seen dogs hunting in the Thames.'

'That's not *that* strange,' Howard said. 'Dogs are good swimmers.'

'Especially when they have fins in the middle of their backs,' said the boy. 'There were butterflies with teeth when the weather got hot too, beautiful things, till they had your ear off. My name's Hubcap by the way.'

Howard smiled, 'Hubcap?'

'Yeah. Got a problem with that?'

'No, course not. I'm Howard.'

'Now *that's* a stupid name.'

'Stupider than Hubcap?'

'Much.'

'Call me Steering Wheel if you prefer.'

'Seat Belt?'

The two boys smiled at one another.

'Hand Brake suits me better.' Howard held up his hands to show him how broken they were.

'Little Chef will fix you up.'

'Who?'

'He's the boss at Potter's Bar, where I live. Come on.'

Hubcap started to march back along the motorway, Howard jogging on behind.

'How far is it?' Howard asked.

'Potter's Bar? Not far, five miles or so as the pigeon flies. We'll get your hands bandaged, something to eat. There's a bed for you too, if you want.'

'I'd love it, if you're sure. I spent last night in the back of a van.' Howard told him about his uncomfortable night and the sounds of the bikers that had kept him awake.

'That sounds like one of Tiger's crews,' Hubcap said. 'They ride up and down at night, supposed to be keeping an eye out but I reckon they don't do much except drink and break stuff.'

'An eye out for what?' Howard asked.

Hubcap looked a little uncomfortable at the question. 'There's worse things out here than pigeons.'

Howard just bet there was.

'So, where were you then?' asked Hubcap.

'Eh?'

'You know, it's what you always ask innit? Where were you when it happened?'

'Oh, that's a bit… difficult.'

'Always is but, y'know, better out than in.'

'No, I mean it's difficult because I have no idea.' Howard could see no harm in telling Hubcap about his lack of memories. 'I woke up in the middle of the road yesterday with no idea who or where I was.'

Hubcap looked at him with disbelief. 'Right…'

'Seriously, I know *things*, like…' He looked around for an example. 'I don't know… all of it, these are cars, that's London, this is… now I'm guessing, the M25?'

'Yes, visitor from beyond the stars, that is what we humans used to call it. '

'*Used* to?'

Hubcap sighed. 'Alright… it's The Perimeter now, as in the closest anyone with half a brain—and this may not include you obviously—will go towards the city.'

'Why?'

Hubcap stopped walking, 'Don't mess with me, ok?'

'I'm not I…' Howard didn't know how he could convince him he was genuine. 'Look I woke up yesterday lying in the middle of the road with a cut on my face—a face I don't even *recognise* by the way, I mean really… not even "that's a bit familiar", y'know? I can't begin to *tell* you how sick that makes me feel. I'm *guessing* my name's Howard because it's written in here,' he pulled the notebook out of his pocket and handed it to Hubcap, 'but I don't *know* it is. I might have just picked the book up somewhere...' Howard took some deep breaths, trying to stay calm.

'I met this guy,' he said. 'He was, I don't know, foreign, Russian... Polish maybe... *whatever*. He was nice, he shared his food with me, gave me a little advice. I woke up this morning to find his head stuck on top of the van I'd been sleeping in.' Hubcap stopped flicking through the notebook and gave Howard his full attention. 'It was just sat there,' Howard continued, 'his beard all... gooey.'

'Jesus, that's sick.' Hubcap handed the notebook back.

'Yeah...' Howard slipped the notebook into his coat pocket. '... Aren't you going to ask me *how* it happened? I mean, isn't that what someone would normally do?' He could feel that mixture of anger and panic building in his chest again.

'Not anymore,' Hubcap replied. 'People turn up dead all the time and there are a hundred and one impossible things out there that could have done it.' He began to walk again. 'And the fact that you don't know *that* is the best proof you could have given me that you only woke up yesterday. Well,' he turned and gave a cheeky grin, 'that and the fact that you decided to give yourself a stupid name like Howard just 'cos you read it in a book.'

Howard smiled back.

'OK,' Hubcap said as they were side by side again. 'I'll tell you where *I* was when it happened because...' he struggled to put the feeling into words '... well, I think it might be important to have a moment like that in your life, something that makes you fit in the world now it's the way it is. Makes sense, yeah?'

'I guess.'

'You not having that moment of your own, I figure you can borrow mine.'

While it was obvious that Hubcap had told the story lots of times, he still took a moment to get his head around it, to swallow the emotion of it and line up the words.

'Like your book says, it was the sixth of January. I was getting ready for school, used to hate that, especially in the winter when it was too dark and cold to do anything but stay in bed. I was having my breakfast, trying to wake up with as much chocolate and sugar as I could ram into my gob. Dad was drinking his coffee... he loved coffee, mum used to give him grief about how much he drank before she ran off with a bloke from her office. Maybe he preferred tea. Anyway... there was this noise from outside, it's hard to describe, a bit like paper tearing but deeper, stronger, y'know? It was a *wrong* sound. You heard it and knew it meant something bad. Dad went to the window and looked out, but there was nothing to see, not in the street.

'Other noises started up, car horns, shouting, glass smashing... all mixed up together. I met a guy once who described it as the theme music for the end of the world. Weird guy.

'Dad went to the front door and I remember thinking it was a bad idea, that I should stop him somehow, tell him to stay inside. I just... I just couldn't think of a way to say it that didn't sound stupid. So I didn't say anything. He walked outside and I watched him through the window. I watched him turn back towards the house and look up. He stared into the sky. His mouth hanging open. He still had his coffee mug in his hand, he dropped it and the coffee sprayed everywhere, all over his shoes and suit trousers. I remember thinking he'd be mad about it, that we'd be late leaving the house as he'd have to change.

'It's his face that I really remember. Your dad's someone strong y'know? He's the guy that you look up to—even when he's driving you mad—the one that you know will always be able to manage, won't get scared, won't panic. Dad's are just *there*, as solid as the house you live in. Maybe that was the lesson I learned from it: Dad's are no different to the rest of us. He was terrified. His eyes were *so* big. He bit down on his lip and I swear I could see blood trickle down his chin, it looked black, not red...'

Howard felt awkward, Hubcap's voice had gone light, and even though he stared at the road ahead, Howard knew he wasn't looking at it, he was seeing his father.

'He just dropped.' Hubcap blinked and looked at Howard, tearing himself away from the memory. 'His legs folded and… he just dropped. I knew he was dead, I know some people think I'm just saying that 'cos I'm ashamed of not running out after him but I really mean it. I knew he was *dead*. There was nothing I could do.

'I stared out of the window for a few more minutes, there were other people who came running out of their houses and they all did the same as my dad, stared up at whatever it was in the sky, panicked and died. There was a street full of 'em by the time the sun came up properly.

'The noise came again, that ripping noise… and I went upstairs, got changed out of my school uniform and just… I don't know… kind of vegged out for a bit. I sat on my dad's bed and just stared into space. Don't know for how long. After a while it sort of clicked that I was sat there and I snapped out of it. I thought I should probably get my dad's body back inside. Don't know why, just seemed the right thing to do.

'I went back downstairs and checked out of the window, a woman went running past with a little kid on her shoulder. She didn't even look at the bodies on the road, just jumped over 'em. I figured that if she could run around out there then so could I.

'When I stepped out of the front door, the sun had come out and the air was really fresh. One of those good winter mornings. That didn't seem right, how could it be so clear, so cool, so *nice?* The world doesn't care what happens on it, it's only in movies that it rains when the good guys die.

'I walked down our path and stood for a minute at our front gate, staring at the bodies dotted about along the road, hoping they'd move, get up and brush themselves down. I knew they wouldn't but… it's just not something the brain knows how to deal with, it tries to convince itself that it's not seeing what it thinks it's seeing.

'I had to force myself off our path. Open the gate and step onto the road, I knew if I didn't get it done then I would end up going back in the house and staying there. Until we ran out of food and I starved to death probably, which, as my dad shopped like an idiot, wouldn't take long. I needed to *just do it.*

'I stepped over the body of one of our neighbours, Julie something… never knew her surname. Dad fancied her and I always used to imagine them ending up together. Guess they did. One of her legs was bent right back, twisted in the fall, looking like a leg never should.

'Dad was pretty normal. If it hadn't been for his face—that look—you might have thought he was sunbathing or something, messing about…

'I tried to pick him up from under his arms and it was ok for a few feet, just dragging him along, but he was a big guy and… well, a dead weight. I didn't want to drag him by his feet, it seemed wrong, disrespectful or something, I just… well, didn't *want* to.

'I kept pulling him along in short bursts, squatting down, hooking my hands under his arms and then back-pedalling as fast as I could.

'It was when I got to the gate that I really had problems.

'I managed to get his shoulders through but then his foot caught on the gatepost and I fell backwards with him landing on top of me

Hubcap looked embarrassed. 'It just set me off. I ended up bawling my bloody eyes out, like a baby…'

'I'd have been just the same,' Howard said.

Hubcap gave one of those cheeky smiles, 'Yeah… maybe you even *were*.' He kicked a pebble along the row of cars, as if to dismiss his previous tears and carried on with his story. 'The strange thing was a switch just flipped in my head. One minute I was lying there hugging him and crying my eyes out, and the next I was just like… *bam!* No more tears, no worrying, *nothing*. I left my dad's body on the path—it's not like it was really him anymore—went back into the house, filled a bag with food and stuff and was on the road in the space of half an hour.'I just walked out of the city, well… no, there was no "just" about it, I saw stuff that'd make your head bleed—but now's not the time to go into all that. Eventually I was picked up by one of Tiger's biker gangs and I've been with 'em ever since.'

There was a slip road just ahead of them, Hubcap pointed at it. 'Nearly there.'

'So,' Howard said, 'let me just get one thing straight. I sort of assumed, what with the state of everything that all this happened ages ago but it was only…'

'Nine months ago, yeah. Time flies when the world's on its arse.'

Chapter Four

THE SERVICE STATION car park had been turned into a mechanic's dream, everywhere you looked there were rows of machine parts and gleaming engines, cars being broken-down or built-up, motorbikes, lorries and coaches.

'This is the Kingdom of Welcome Break,' Hubcap chuckled, 'hope you're good with a spanner.'

'I've got on alright with *you* so far.'

'Ha ha,' Hubcap gave Howard a punch on the arm. 'Most of the people here are petrol-heads; you get used to the constant noise.'

Howard would have to trust him on that, right now the revving of engines and clang of metal against metal was deafening.

Beyond the car park was a set of large buildings: a petrol station, hotel and the central complex of shops and restaurants. That's where they headed. Hubcap waved at a few people as they went by. They all wore long hair and beards, rough leather and boots; they looked like a cross between normal bikers and mediaeval knights.

One giant of a man waved the spout of an oxyacetylene torch at them and gave an enthusiastic roar.

'That's Tank,' Hubcap explained, 'he's off his head. Completely.'

'Good friend of yours, is he?'

Hubcap punched him on the arm again. 'You're getting a bit too cheeky for your own good. He is a good mate, yeah. He's even better mates with Tiger though, if you know what I mean?' Hubcap gave a wink and walked in a camp way for a few steps.

'Oh...'

'Yep.'

'They're...?'

'Oh yes.'

'Ah.'

'Totally.'

Howard shrugged. 'Fair enough, doesn't bother me.'

'You'd be surprised, it bothers some. The world's ended and people still have time to worry about who's doing stuff to what. Mental.'

They stepped inside the main building and the sound of machinery was swapped for the fanfares of a large amusement arcade. A group of bikers cheered as one of their number got a high score smacking at plastic crocodiles with a big sponge mallet.

'Everyone needs a hobby,' Hubcap said with a smile.

After the amusement arcade was an empty-looking

shop. 'The chocolate and porn went months ago,' Hubcap warned, 'but there's still a few books and magazines if you like that sort of thing. Just put 'em back when you're done so someone else can have a look.'

To their left was a large food court, lots of different fast-food counters and a more traditional looking cafeteria.

'Don't get horny for a Big Mac,' said Hubcap, 'the burgers went ages ago. There's a team of lads that keep the main café going though, mostly tinned stuff of course but they do their best.'

'Is it all blokes?' Howard asked.

'Nah... mostly, but there's a few women about. The doctor's a woman.'

'What's her name? Stethoscope? Thermometer?'

'Val, actually, and if you keep flapping your gob like that I'll make sure you *really* need to see her.'

'Nice.'

Val ran her surgery from what had been a small chemist's at the far end of the main building. She was a big woman whose wavy red hair sprayed out from her face to give her a look of constant surprise. She had a very bad bedside manner:

'Bloody hell!' she shouted, looking at Howard's hands, 'what have you been doing, using a cheese grater as a punch-bag?'

He told her about the pigeons.

'Dear God,' she replied, rummaging through a box

for some antiseptic cream, 'I'm right not to leave the compound by the sounds of it.' She leaned over to Howard as if telling him a big secret. 'I have allergies... five minutes outside and I'd be scratching like a stray dog.'

'Oh,' Howard replied, not knowing what else to say.

'''E's got... *whatyoumacallit*... amnesia as well.' Hubcap said. 'Woke up yesterday in the middle of the road and hasn't got the foggiest how he got there. Didn't know nothing about The Change and that.'

'Really?' Val seemed fascinated.

Howard shrugged. He supposed it hardly mattered if everyone knew. 'I only know what Hubcap's told me.'

'So what's that all about then?' asked Hubcap.

'Depends what type of amnesia it is,' Val replied. 'If it was caused by some kind of physical injury—a bump on the head or whatever—then it would be what we call post-traumatic amnesia.' She poked at Howard's head, probing through his hair and checking his scalp. 'You have a graze on your forehead but it doesn't look like much.'

'What other types are there?' Howard asked.

'Dissociative amnesia, brought on by psychological trauma.'

'Being a bit spazzed in the brain?' Hubcap asked.

Val gave him a dirty look. '"Spazzed" is not a medical term, and we've all had our fair share of psychological trauma these last few months haven't we? Dissociative amnesia is usually the brain's way of locking off a certain period of time in order to save itself from the unpleasant memory.' She began bandaging Howard's hands. 'What can you remember from before The Change?'

'Nothing at all.' Howard admitted. 'I know where I am and what stuff is, but nothing about myself.'

'Global amnesia,' Val nodded, 'which is as rare as rocking horse turds outside of movies and video-games.'

'Cool,' Hubcap grinned, 'you've got something *rare*. Go you!'

'Thanks for the support, mate,' Howard replied. 'So what am I supposed to do about it?' he asked Val.

'Not much you *can* do to be honest, love,' she said, tying off his bandages. 'Your memory will either come back or it won't. It could do it tomorrow or in five years' time. I know it must be scary, but you're a blank slate; free to start again; build a whole new you. Some would say that's a blessing.'

'Thank you for that Doctor Valerie,' said Hubcap in a posh voice. 'One last thing, my friend's name is "Howard". Is there anything medically that can be done about *that*?'

Howard slapped him on the back of the head and then winced as his bandaged hand throbbed.

Chapter Five

AFTER LEAVING DOCTOR Val, Hubcap led Howard out of the building and over to the motel. The foyer was empty. Hubcap marched up to the desk and began banging on the little bell that sat in the counter.

'Nobody'll come,' he admitted, 'I just like the noise.' He walked past the counter, pulled a small card from a drawer and passed it to Howard. 'That's your key, some boff's fixed it so that all the cards open all the doors. You'll be sharing with me but, y'know, so's you've got your own.'

'Thanks.'

'You won't thank me by the time we've walked it, the lift's knackered.'

It was three flights and several fire doors before they found themselves at the door of 311.

'What did I tell you?' moaned Hubcap, 'you're ready for a few hours kip by the time you get here.'

The door was decorated with a big Spider-Man poster. 'Like comics, eh?' Howard asked.

'See, there you go with that global amnesia thing, doesn't

know his own shoe size but can spot a Peter Parker when he sees one. Love 'em, yeah. And if you don't remember your feelings on the subject then let's just say you do too shall we? Last thing I need is a roommate who takes the mick.'

Howard grinned, 'I can't get enough web-slinging action.'

'Cool. I picked up a bunch from the shop downstairs but not many, used to have loads, proper American ones. Nobody has much of anything anymore though.' He swiped his keycard in the lock and opened the door. 'Make yourself at home, what's mine is... well, *mine*, but I guess you can look at it longingly if you want.'

It was dark inside, the curtains were drawn and Howard could tell nothing about the room beyond the fact that if he wanted to walk in it, he would have to kick dirty clothes as he went.

'Sorry,' Hubcap said, 'I never open the curtains, I work best with the lights.'

He flicked them on and Howard was taken back enough to audibly draw breath.

The walls were covered with drawings. Black and white mostly, done with pencil and marker pen, though every now and then there would be something in full colour.

'I suppose it's my version of that book of yours,' Hubcap said, 'emptying my head.'

Howard recognised Hubcap in most of the drawings:

here he was dragging his father along the pavement, running along the roofs of cars, being chased by something that looked an awful lot like an angry vacuum cleaner...

'That was a fun day,' Hubcap smiled, noticing the picture Howard was looking at, 'Remind me to tell you about the Terrible Cleaning Crew of Tottenham Cemetery one day, freaky lot they were...'

'It's your very own comic book.'

'Yeah, *The Spectacular Adventures of Hubcap*,' he gave a sideways glance. 'I know, the title needs work...'

'The rest doesn't!' Howard ran his eyes across a selection of panels that showed Hubcap hunting a rat among the rows of stationary cars they had recently left. 'Seriously, these are brilliant.'

'Yeah, well... one day I'll have some paper and decent ink then I can do them properly. It's hard to lend a wall to someone to see what they think of it.'

'They're just... amazing.' Howard was beginning to lose himself in the narratives he found, following story panels with his index finger and tracing Hubcap's journey from his home to Potters Bar.

He was still reading them a couple of hours later when Hubcap dragged him away to go and get some food. 'It's banquet night tonight,' he explained, 'we do it once a week, so that everybody can get together, have a bit of laugh.'

The atmosphere in the car park had changed, people

had stopped working and started *playing*. There was a picnic area beyond the petrol station and this had been set-up as a jousting arena. Riders roared as they charged their bikes at one another. Howard's nose was tickled by the sharp smell of petrol as a man juggled flaming torches to the hoots of his crowd. They paused at a table where a man moved cards around at speed, challenging all comers to 'Find the Lady'. Most watching were as distracted as the two boys by the lady found on the *back* of the pornographic cards. No wonder the man shuffling them never lost.

'Hubcap!' They turned to see Tank waving at them. He was holding a large sledgehammer and had something strapped to his chest.

'Here we go,' Hubcap sighed, 'he and Tiger are always coming up with something mad for banquet nights.'

They strolled over to watch. Tank was playing to the crowd, limbering-up and raising his slabs of hands to laughs and encouragement. He waved the boys to the front.

'Away you go there, lad,' he said in a thick Scottish accent, 'you dinnae wanna miss this. Who's your wee pal there?'

'He's new, found 'im out on The Perimeter.'

Howard introduced himself and Tank took his hand and squeezed it just shy of breaking point. 'Good to meet you lad, the name's Douggie but these daft sods call me Tank.'

'What's that about then?' asked Hubcap, pointing at Tank's chest where a breeze block had been tied to a dustbin lid, the whole lot strapped over his shoulders.

'That, lad, is the ultimate in banquet night entertainment!' This last had been shouted at the top of his voice to another roar from the crowd. 'May I introduce you to the man that was knocking them dead even before The Change, the man they call... *the Tiger!*'

Tiger appeared with a high pitched whoop. He was wearing a devil outfit that was far too small for him, the cape finishing in the middle of his back. He grabbed the sledgehammer from Tank and raised it above his head. The crowd began to clap a rhythm and Tiger danced, hopping a jig and punching the sledgehammer in the air.

'Now,' Tank continued, holding up a walnut, 'allow us to present to you the most lethal nutcracker you will ever see!' The crowd laughed. 'I shall take this tasty walnut and...'

Tiger swung the sledgehammer at Tank's chest and sent the big man flying. The breeze-block snapped in two and the walnut flew into the air. Tank lay flat on his back while Tiger recommenced his jig to the laughs of the crowd.

Howard and Hubcap ran over to the prone Tank.

'You alright Tank?' Hubcap asked, trying to unhook the dustbin lid from the man's chest.

'I think the timing needs a little work,' Tank whispered, 'better leave the lid, it might be the only thing keeping me lungs in. I dinnae suppose you'd fetch Val would ye? I think I might need to have a little word with her.'

'Oh…' Hubcap stopped fussing with the straps, 'yeah, of course we'll fetch her now.'

'Aye, no rush lad, I'm no' going anywhere…'

Howard raised his eyebrows at Hubcap and the two of them went off towards the main building.

Tiger and Tank weren't alone in their unconventional attempts to provide entertainment. Two burly gents in tutus pirouetted to a classical CD with all the grace of elephants caught in machine-gun fire. A woman in a top hat accidentally stabbed her 'glamourous assistant' as he crammed himself into a glittery cabinet on her behalf—the stabbing was not fatal, but it certainly killed the act. An elderly lady was trying to spin plates on slender poles. The act was all the more watchable given her inability to do so: watching someone spin pates is boring, watching an hysterical pensioner surrounded by shattering dinnerware is quite a laugh.

'Tank needs seeing to,' Hubcap shouted to Val as they spotted her in the plate-spinner's crowd.

'Oh, I'm sure I'm going to be needed here in a minute too,' she took a last look at the old lady before running off towards the far edge of the car park. 'Save me from banquet nights,' she shouted over her shoulder, 'I just can't cope.'

Howard and Hubcap walked around the crowds for

awhile, watching bits of the acts until a loud siren drew everyone's attention. Howard peered past the milling bikers to see a tiny man swinging the same kind of tube that Hubcap had used on the pigeons. He had to stand on a box to give himself enough room to swing the pipe.

'That's Little Chef,' Hubcap said, 'or "Mini Me" if you really want him to punch you in the 'nads."

'Grub's up!' Little Chef shouted, and the crowd roared.

'Get moving,' Hubcap shouted, 'unless you want to get trampled to death, this lot get hungry.'

Everyone marched into the main building, grabbed their trays and started forming queues at the restaurant's heated counter. The food was an assortment of different coloured slops, beans, chilli, curry, Alphabetti Spaghetti… anything tinned. Behind the counter stood a man in white overalls who looked like a slightly more youthful Father Christmas.

'Good evening Ladies and Gentlemen!' he announced. 'May I particularly recommend the "All Day Breakfast"? Its reconstituted bacon-flavour strips are particularly delicious today.'

There was a ripple of laughter. Howard chose a plate of macaroni cheese and moved further down the line.

'Now then!' Hubcap grinned. 'Banquet night means puddings!'

There was a choice of steamed sponges: chocolate, jam or golden syrup. Howard went for the chocolate, while Hubcap demanded a scoop of all three.

'You'll be sick.' Howard said. Hubcap planned on attacking a dungheap of chili and meatballs before he even got close to the soup of sponge and custard.

'Never, there's not a pudding in the word that can beat me, I am King of Puddings.'

The tables had been set out in long rows like a mediaeval banquet, with space left in the middle for a rough stage of wooden pallets. Howard and Hubcap sat down in the corner where they would still have a good view but weren't too close to the front. The seats filled up quickly, but nobody started their food, waiting for everybody to gather. Howard was relieved to see Tank limp in supported by Tiger. He looked tender but at least he was mobile. Once everyone had sat down, Little Chef climbed up onto his chair at the head of the central table and held out his hands for silence.

No more than four foot, he nonetheless towered over those around him with his personality. His blonde hair was tied in a ponytail and he wore a layered leather and chain-mail outfit that made him look like a Viking.

'It's alright,' he said, 'I'm not going to waffle on, with all due respect to our devoted chefs, this crap tastes bad enough when hot, so God help us if it goes cold.' There was plenty of laughter at that and the man in the chef's whites stuck his middle finger up at the room. 'I just wanted to take this opportunity to welcome a new face at our table.' He pointed over towards Howard who swallowed nervously as the room's eyes fell on him. 'Our good friend Hubcap found Howard on The Perimeter and brought him safely here to us.'

'Sorry mate,' Hubcap whispered out of the corner of his mouth, 'it's nothing to do with me, Val must have told 'im.'

'Of course,' Little Chef continued, 'what Howard doesn't know is that we're all mad psychos desperate for the taste of fresh meat and that we fully intend to kill him in his bed so that we can feast on his innards tomorrow night.'

Little Chef grabbed a knife from beside his plate, jumped on the table and ran towards Howard with a growl. The room erupted in a roar and Howard fell backwards over his chair as Little Chef stood either side of his dinner and held the knife up in the air. Then he burst into a fit giggles.

'Sorry mate,' he said between breaths, 'I never can resist doing that one.' Everyone in the room started laughing as Hubcap helped Howard back onto his feet. Little Chef patted him on the shoulder. 'Welcome, you're amongst friends. We're mad as a bucket of frog's eyes, but our hearts are in the right place.'

He walked back towards his own seat. 'Go on then,' he shouted, 'get it down you.' He jumped back onto his chair and began to scoop spaghetti hoops into his mouth.

'That was... freaky.' Howard said as he poked at his macaroni. 'Anyone else likely to run at me with a knife, or shall I get on with my dinner?'

'You should be safe,' Hubcap mumbled around a meatball. 'Told you they were a bit mad, didn't I?'

'Yeah… guess you did.'

Howard managed to eat the rest of his meal in peace, though he did get chatting with the couple sat next to him as he polished off his chocolate sponge. The man wore a frizzy perm and dark, round sunglasses, the woman had a crew-cut which made her features all the softer.

'Where were you then?' the man asked in a thick Midlands accent.

'Eh?' It took Howard a second to remember the custom. 'Oh… I don't know, sorry I have…' he tried to remember the precise expression Val had used, 'global amnesia.'

'Oh, right… bummer.'

'Doesn't sound too bad to me,' the woman said. She gave Howard a smile to show she wasn't meaning to be cruel. He had already realised that most people would envy the fact that he couldn't remember The Change.

'How about you?' he asked.

'We'd just flown in to Stanstead,' she said, 'two weeks in Malaga—Jerry likes the sun.'

'No point in a holiday without a bit of sun,' the man agreed. 'Sally here seems to think you can't have culture *and* a tan.'

'We were just heading out of the airport, trying to remember where we left the car,' Sally continued, ignoring Jerry.

'You'll notice she says "we" there as if it wasn't actually her—the driver—that had lost the car.'

'*Whatever...*' Sally rolled here eyes, these two were obviously always like this, there was no malice in it. 'I was on the floor, going through my handbag trying to find the ticket when we heard the noise, y'know that sort of ripping noise?'

'Yeah, I know what you mean.'

'I felt it right away,' Jerry said. 'It's hard to describe... it was if the world was being displaced by this thing appearing, like water rippling away when you throw a rock into a pond. I could feel it on my face... the world... *rippling*. I grabbed Sally and held her face against my shoulder.'

'My hero!' Sally smiled, stroking Jerry's hand. 'Of course at the time I was fighting to look, I couldn't understand why he wouldn't let me.'

'I didn't really know either,' Jerry added, 'it was just, like, instinct or something.'

'But how come it didn't affect you?' Howard asked.

'C'mon kid,' Jerry said pulling his glasses down to show his pale, blind eyes, 'you didn't think I was enough of a tit to be wearing these inside without a reason did you?'

Howard was suitably embarrassed. 'Oh, sorry... I didn't think...'

Sally chuckled. 'Ignore him, he just likes making people uncomfortable.'

'So,' Howard was eager to change the subject, 'how did you end up here then?'

'We got stuck in the traffic like everyone else, eventually decided there was no point in sitting in a queue till something did for us. I mean... did you *see* the cars?'

'Yeah.'

'It was horrible, so many people just locked their doors and sat there, starved to death... they just sat and *died*.'

'I keep telling her,' Jerry interrupted, '"after effect", wasn't it? Some took longer than others is all, something happened that most people couldn't deal with, some died straight away—the ones that saw it—others took a few hours, like it was waiting in their heads, ready to make 'em just...' He mimed the flicking of a switch. 'That's what The Change was, not just the few minutes in the sky but all the stuff that followed after, the stuff that *keeps* happening... we are being thinned out, exterminated.'

'Shut up Jerry!' This was not what Sally wanted to hear.

'Sorry...' Jerry didn't have it in him to push the point, he loved her too much. 'Ignore me, I go on sometimes.'

Sally got to her feet and walked out, partly through anger, partly through embarrassment. Jerry heard her go and stood up carefully.

Howard felt this was partly his fault somehow. 'Do you want me to...?'

Jerry held up his hand. 'No kid, it's alright. I can manage. I know this place well enough to get out without breaking my neck. I'm slower, but that's no bad thing. She might have calmed down by the time I get to her.'

'Embarrassing,' Howard said to Hubcap who was slowly trying to poke more of his pudding mountain into his mouth. Hubcap looked at Howard, a ring of custard and chocolate sauce around his lips and did his best to reply without spraying the table with sponge. The result was a half-shrug/half-grunt.

Things were about to get worse. Once everyone had finished eating Little Chef got to his feet again and announced that evening's entertainment, none other than 'Mystifying Molly and her Beautiful Assistant Derek.'

This turned out to be the rather embarrassing magician from outside. The glamorous Derek, in sequins and a smile, was now sporting a large dressing where Molly had accidentally stabbed him.

'Good evening, Ladies and Gentlemen,' Molly shouted, striding into the space in the middle of the tables, 'prepare to be amazed!'

'Why?' asked Hubcap, having finally swallowed his sponge, 'is she going to get a trick right?'

She carried on, 'Tonight I shall astound you not with cabinets and swords, playing cards and rope but, instead, something far more natural and yet... terrifying!'

'Please tell me she's not going to strip,' Hubcap whispered. 'I'll upchuck my meatballs if I see so much as a bra strap I swear.'

Howard giggled but immediately had to stifle it as Molly pointed at him.

'If I may ask our new arrival to join me,' she said, 'he will be of great assistance.' The room burst into applause as Howard bit his lip in embarrassment and got to his feet.

'I thank you!' she said, taking him by his hand and encouraging him to take his applause. 'Now, tonight we are going to explore one of the deepest and darkest natural secrets together…' Howard caught a glimpse of Hubcap in hysterics at this and immediately looked away, not wanting to get the giggles. 'We are going to plummet the shadowy recesses of nothing less than the human mind!'

The bikers gave a cheer.

Molly gave a little bow before continuing. 'Derek, bring on the Mentalizer!'

Howard couldn't help but laugh then. "The Mentalizer"? What the hell was that?

Derek shuffled on with a sigh, pushing a large object covered in a black cloth.

'Ladies and Gentlemen,' continued Molly, 'the Mentalizer is the very peak of scientific achievement. It is a miracle of fine engineering and computer technology. With this machine I can make a man's imagination reality.'

She whipped the black cloth off to reveal a rather sorry looking contraption. A stool surrounded by various wires, circuits and an ancient-looking computer monitor. There was also what may once have been a colander but was now intended to be a skull cap, a spaghetti of wiring sprouting from the bowl and vanishing into the 'machine'. There was a wave of laughter as the audience took it all in.

'Don't worry, kid,' Molly whispered in his ear, 'my toothbrush is more technical than this thing, just play along, ok?'

Howard gave her a slight nod.

'When I wire-up our willing victim… oh I'm sorry, I mean "volunteer".' Nobody laughed but she gave the gag a pause anyway. 'I will be able to take the dreams from his mind and make them appear—as real—before your very eyes.'

There was a half-mocking 'ooh' from the audience as she sat Howard on the stool and dropped the colander on his head.

'First what I need to do,' she continued, 'is to build the psychic atmosphere of the room.'

'I had the beans,' Tiger shouted, 'will that help?'

Everyone laughed, except Mystifying Molly who pretended he hadn't said anything at all. 'What we need to do is link our minds together so the energies resonate with the psychic plane.'

'Oh yeah…' someone shouted, '*that.*'

'If you could all stand-up please,' Molly said, 'and then link hands.'

There were a few grumbles and moans, but everyone got up and did as she'd asked.

'Right... close your eyes...'

Little Chef laughed. 'I think I begin to see how this trick might be done!' There were a few laughs. 'Check your wallets after!'

Molly ignored him. 'Now we begin to hum...'

'I knew the beans would come into it somewhere...' whispered Tank.

Molly and Derek began to hum, along with a few giggles the rest of the room followed suit.

Molly turned to Howard, whispering under the humming crowd. 'All we do is make a big fuss, a few loud noises and then wheel out a the trolly of beer you're "dreaming" of. They'll love it. You sit there and look as surprised as the rest of 'em, OK?'

'OK.'

The humming grew louder and louder as people started to get into it, nudging one another and trying to outdo others for volume.

The colander on Howard's head twitched. He looked around, panicking that he was about to be electrocuted by the damn thing. Then he realised there was no way of plugging it in, so there was no power in it. The colander twitched again.

'Excuse me...' he hissed at Molly, trying to be subtle on her behalf. She didn't hear him. 'Excuse me...'

The stool suddenly rocked and he grabbed at the metal frame to stop himself falling over. His hands clenched as power surged through him. He tried to let go but his fists wouldn't open. The entire frame began rocking, the wires thrashing, the computer monitor turned on, its screen filled with static.

Molly just stared, at a loss what to do. The humming stopped as people became aware something was going on. For a few seconds people just watched, perhaps thinking this was all part of the show.

It was Tiger who responded first.

'Get him out of there!' he shouted, vaulting over the table and running towards Howard. The frame began to glow and before Tiger could reach it a bolt of electricity shot impossibly from one of the circuit boards and sent him thrashing to the floor.

'Turn it off!' Little Chef shouted.

'There's nothing *to* turn off!' Derek replied, 'I mean, seriously... the thing hasn't even got a battery.'

'Oh yeah?' Tiger groaned, 'that'll be why my knackers are smoking, will it?'

Hubcap stood as close as he dared, trying to think of something he could do, but having seen what had happened to Tiger nobody really wanted to risk getting closer.

'I'm alright,' Howard shouted, 'I think... it doesn't hurt or anything, I just can't...'

The static had vanished from the monitor, replaced by a pulsing web of flesh, like the footage you see in surgery when they insert tiny cameras into people. The screen began to bubble as if composed of thick liquid before swelling out of the frame. Like an inflated balloon it grew larger and larger. The crowd began to move back, Howard trying to pull himself as far away from it as possible.

It exploded. A thick black tentacle of flesh, a fat cousin to the things Howard had seen inside the pigeons, burst out and began thrashing from side to side. The gathered bikers ducked as it whistled past them, the suckers on its side revolving like tiny buzz saws.

Hubcap grabbed a knife from the table behind him and swung at it but the tentacle just smacked him across the room. More and more lightning bolts shot from the machine, exploding in a shower of sparks off the roof and the walls. One fat biker was sent flying, landing on a table and catapulting plates and cutlery into the crowd. The tentacle thrashed harder and harder until suddenly it simply vanished, leaving Howard, now free, to collapse unconscious to the floor.

'Well,' said Little Chef as everybody got back to their feet, 'that's the best turn we've had on banquet banquet night for *weeks*.'

Chapter Six

'SALLY?' JERRY COULD smell her perfume so he knew she was close. Even though the car-park reeked of motor oil (and a sweet, rotting odour that he couldn't place, like meat past its prime) he would always recognise that smell. He'd bought the perfume himself, she had insisted he choose it for her. 'You may not be able to *see* how gorgeous I am,' she had joked, 'but you're always going to love the way I smell.'

He held out his hand, certain that she was within reach. He tapped his cane gently on the tarmac, not wanting to hit her with it but determined to know she was there. 'Sally?'

She wouldn't make him chase her all over the place, she wouldn't be that cruel.

'Sally?' His fingers brushed her cheek. 'Sally! I'm sorry...' There was a dampness on her face. 'Have you been crying? Oh I'm so sorry...' He rubbed the wet between his fingers, surely it was too thick for tears? 'Sally?'

There was the hiss of hydraulic motors and the thing that had been stood there all along, holding Sally's head up for Jerry to find, grabbed the blind man by the throat and began to poke and prod his body for things of interest.

In the end all it left were the eyes.

Chapter Seven

HOWARD WAS BACK on the road, standing between the rows of vehicles. The light was fading from the sky leaving the slightly unreal quality of dusk. He was unable to move, which scared him as he knew that something was coming up behind him, he could hear the noise its puffy fat limbs made as they scraped along the dusty tarmac. He could hear the wheeze of a hydraulic engine too, pistons pumping, steam whistling. Closer it came until he could nearly feel its chipped and bloody nails on the back of his neck. A rush of images flashed into his head: the frontage of the main restaurant building exploding in a shower of glass as something burst through it; the thick smell of petrol crawling into his nose while someone sang close-by; the rev of a motorbike engine and a spark of flame. He heard a voice, 'Adrian,' it said, 'now there's a name that tastes familiar.' Then he was somewhere else entirely, walking along a smaller road towards the centre of London. Hubcap whistled tunelessly next to him.

Howard began to slip out of his body, floating up and

up until he was looking down on himself, walking side by side with his new friend. From above the shops and houses he could see the people lying in wait for them but had no voice with which to give a warning. He watched as he and Hubcap were swamped by the gang of savages, heard his own shouts as a makeshift spear was jabbed towards his throat and his hands were tied behind his back.

Then he was gone again, this time to find himself sprawled face-first in mud, sweat dripping down the back of his neck from the humid air around him. All around him leaves and branches curled of their own volition, writhing towards him...

Then he was running along the white-tiled corridors of the Underground, the sounds of pursuit close behind...

Then he was up to his neck in cold water, the roar of an unearthly creature echoing over the waves...

The images kept coming, faster and faster. Were they premonitions or memories? Certainly they were not dreams, they were far too clear, too *perfect* for that.

He woke beneath The Spectacular Adventures of Hubcap and the pictures seemed mild compared to the visions in his own head.

Their artist was staring at him from the foot of the bed.

'You alright?' he said. 'I was brickin' it.'

'Yeah...' Howard replied, 'I think. What happened?'

'Erm... dunno to be honest, nobody does... things went boom... tentacles... you sparko. Val having a panic attack until she decides you're not actually dead...erm...' He shrugged. 'That's about the sum total of my knowledge, mate, it's beyond me I'm afraid. You killed the party though, most people called it an early night. Remind me never to invite you to my birthday.'

'Tentacles...'

'Yeah, weird huh?'

'Yeah.' A thought from when he had been unconscious burst out. 'I'm not supposed to stay here.'

'Eh? Nobody blames you mate.'

'No,' Howard shook his head, 'I don't mean it like that, the thing is I'm supposed to walk into London.'

'Who says?' Hubcap scoffed.

'I don't know, I can't explain it, I just know it's what I'm supposed to do. I need to go into London.'

'What for?'

'No idea.'

'I can give you a few suggestions if you like, having been there... there's the Tower of course, the London Eye... what else? Oh yes, dying horribly as something *really* nasty tears you to pieces! The city's mad, mate! Nobody in their right mind would go there.'

'I know, that's what makes the other thing difficult...'

'"Other thing"?'

'Yeah,' Howard looked at Hubcap, the awkwardness plain on his face, 'you're supposed to come with me.'

'Jog on.'

'Seriously.'

Hubcap turned away, kicking a discarded pair of boxer shorts against the wall in irritation. 'Tapped in the head...' he muttered under his breath.

'I know it sounds stupid,' Howard said, 'and I don't know *how* I know it... I just do. There's a reason why I'm here, why I woke up on the road yesterday, why I met you... there's a reason for all of it.'

Hubcap shook his head, 'Be telling me he's the son of God next...'

'I'm sorry, I know it's...'

Hubcap held his hands up. 'Just drop it for now, yeah? We'll talk about it tomorrow.' He walked out of the room muttering, 'By then hopefully the voices in his head will have shut up.'

Chapter Eight

HUBCAP TOOK THE stairs a couple at a time, slapping out his frustration on the banister and wall as he worked his way towards the ground floor. It was his own stupid fault for getting his hopes up. As much as he liked the people here at the Kingdom of Welcome Break, he had been excited at the thought of finding someone his own age, a mate to hang with who wasn't twenty years older than he was and covered in hair. Not much to ask, was it?

He crashed through the main doors and stomped his way back towards the main building.

Just stepping out of the main door were Tiger and Tank, Tank still moving awkwardly from his accident earlier.

'You broken something?' Hubcap shouted.

'His reputation as a hard man,' Tiger joked, 'nothing else apparently.'

'Next time *I'm* having the sledgehammer,' Tank grumbled, 'we'll see how *you* manage, laddie.'

Suddenly Tank slipped and both he and Tiger fell to the ground with a grunt.

'Great,' Tiger muttered, 'now you're making *me* look like an idiot.'

'It's not my fault,' Tank complained, 'there's something all over the ground... gimme some light here.'

Tiger reached into his pocket for a Zippo lighter which he handed to Tank. Tank lit it and held the flame up to his hand, which was wet with blood.

'Jesus...' Tiger panicked, 'what have you done?'

'It's not me.' Tank replied.

'But you're covered in...'

'It's. *Not. Me.*' Tank hovered the lighter over the ground and they could see they were both sat in a pool of blood.

Behind them a couple more people stepped out of the main building.

'Oi!' Tiger shouted to them, holding up his hands, 'we need some help here. Get some proper lights and a group of lads, someone's been hurt.'

Chapter Nine

HOWARD SIGHED, GOT off the bed and walked over to the window. It was never going to have been easy was it? He might *know* that he had to trust in his gut and make the journey into the city (in fact it was the only thing he *did* know since waking up the day before) but convincing someone else that they should come with him... based on what evidence? I saw it in a *dream*, mate... good enough for you?

He was lucky Hubcap hadn't chinned him.

He pressed his nose against the glass and looked for the lights of the city in the distance. Maybe this was why he had amnesia, if he really *knew* how bad things could be in the city, he probably wouldn't have the balls to go there.

Suddenly his stomach cramped and he grabbed the windowsill to steady himself. The portion of his dream where he had been frozen to the spot returned to him. He could hear the sound of the creature dragging itself over the grit of the road, hear the thrust and hiss of valves. What sort of vehicle was it riding? What could make the ground shake so much beneath his feet? It was getting closer... a waft of hot air passed across the back of his neck, bringing with it the smell of barbecued meat and engine oil. He screwed his eyes shut and prepared to feel its hand on his shoulder. It didn't come. Opening his eyes and looking down onto the darkened car park, he realised he knew something else: the creature he kept imagining was real and, to make things worse, it was down *there*.

Chapter Ten

TIGER AND TANK were on their feet now, a small group gathering around with torches. Hubcap was trying to see what the cause of the blood could be but, even in the glow of the torch beams, there was nothing to be found. The blood was plentiful, the sticky pool spread for some distance, but there was no body to go with it.

''ang on...' Tiger grabbed one of the torches and shone it along the kerb. 'I think I saw something...*urggh*!'

Little Chef appeared, dropped to his haunches and picked up the object that had disgusted Tiger. Hubcap couldn't tell what it was; ignition keys maybe? There was something dangling from a fatter, rounder object. One of the other bikers shone his torch directly on Little Chef's hand so everyone could see what he was holding: an eyeball.

There was silence for a second.

'When did anybody last see Jerry?' Little Chef asked.

'Erm...' Hubcap pushed his way to the front. 'I saw him at dinner... I... how do you know it was...?' He saw the milky pupil for a second before Little Chef cupped his hand around the eye. 'Oh... he had an argument with Sally, she stormed out and he went running after her.'

'OK.' Little Chef pocketed the eyeball and raised his voice to address everyone. 'We need to get organised. Don't ask me what happened here, because I don't know. What I *do* know is it won't happen to anyone else without a fight.' He turned to Tiger. 'Get your crews on the ball, I want them making sweeps of this place. If what did this is still here, we find *it* before it finds us and we go on the offensive. Everybody else gathers in one place—the banquet hall—bedrolls and safety in numbers. Hubcap?'

'Yeah?'

'Motel run, I want you banging on every door, making sure everyone is out of there. How's the new kid?'

'OK, I think.'

'Good, get him out of there as well. You OK with that?'

'On it.' Hubcap ran back towards the motel.

Chapter Eleven

ONCE ITS THOUGHTS had been clearer, it was pretty sure of that. Clean and simple. Now it's mind was a rattling jar of fragments, a scattershot of urges, colours and sounds that got more confusing day after day. The only way to exist in the chaos was to follow instinct, don't challenge, don't question, just *do*.

It felt wind in its gut from the hasty meal it had snatched in the shadows of the car park. A drive-through snack just to take the edge off. It expelled a hot trickle of reflux from the corner of its mouth and poked a finger at the aching lump in its belly.

It ran a split, yellow nail over the freshest of its wounds, probing the wet flesh and estimating a healing time. Not long, a couple of minutes perhaps for a perfect join.

Its stomach rumbled, acid juices fizzing. It was *so* hungry.

It explored the smells surrounding it, its mouths watering at the scent of sweat and leather that was so close-by. It was no good, it must eat. No rushed snacks though, it would have to engineer a little privacy…

The Change

It stretched out its long fingers and explored the possibilities... ah... *yes*... that should do it...

Chapter Twelve

IN THE BANQUET hall a handful of stragglers were finishing cans of beer and conversations. The 'Glamorous Derek' wasn't living up to his name, he had his feet up on the table and was putting as much alcohol into his mouth as the limited time allowed.

'Never seen anything like it,' he muttered.

'We know,' Mystifying Molly replied. She was getting sick of his repeating the fact.

'So,' Liquid Len—so called because he liked a drink or two—asked, 'you swear you had nothing to do with that?'

'Course not,' Molly replied. 'We were all ready to wheel the beer out, it was just a bit of a joke wasn't it?'

'Beer?' Liquid Len asked. 'You've got beer?'

'You're drinking it.'

'Oh…' Len looked at the can in his hand, 'so I am, most kind…'

There was a pause as everybody around the table took a mouthful of their drinks.

'So, what do we think it was?' asked a thin and haggard

man they called Roll-Up due to his tobacco intake and wrinkled, yellow appearance.

'Who knows these days?' answered the giant known as Beef. 'It's all gone weird. I gave up trying to understand stuff months ago.'

'Yeah,' said Roll-Up, '*weird*.'

'What you want to be asking,' said the big, blonde woman they all knew as Sidecar (as she was always hanging off motorbikes), 'is whether that thing's coming back.'

''No way of telling, is there?' Beef replied.

'I reckon Little Chef should kick the kid out,' Sidecar said, 'just in case. It could be inside *him* for all we know.'

'Won't happen.' Molly muttered.

'How do we know he didn't bring it in here with him?' Sidecar asked.

'We don't,' Molly replied. 'I'm just saying Little Chef won't kick the kid out, he's not like that.'

'Well, maybe he should be...'

'Can't just blame the kid,' Roll-Up argued, 'you saw him, poor sod was right out of it.'

'Oh!' Liquid Len suddenly said. 'I've just had a terrible thought!'

'I knew it,' said Sidecar, 'what?'

Liquid Len held his can up. 'Is there any more beer once we've drunk this lot?'

'Idiot,' Molly sighed. 'Can we just talk about something else?'

'Never seen anything like it,' said Derek.

Molly was on her feet and about to punch him when they were all distracted by the sounds of shouting from outside.

'What's up now?' she muttered, strolling towards the exit of the restaurant just as the metal security shutters that separated it from the rest of the building began to drop.

'They're only locking us in!' she shouted, making a run for the closing gap. She scooted under the shutter just in time, hearing it clatter shut behind her. 'What are they playing at?' 'Probably safer locked in here,' Sidecar said, 'at least we know the kid isn't in here with us.'

The lights went out.

'Brilliant', said Beef. 'Perfect, that is.'

'What's the matter?' said Roll-Up. 'You scared of the dark, big man?'

Beef was but would never admit it. 'After what we saw earlier I'm not happy sitting *anywhere* if I can't see what's going on around me,' he said. 'We should shift over by one of the drinks fridges.' The chiller cabinets, being on a different circuit, were still switched on and shedding pools of light.

'I don't know what you're getting all jittery about,' Len slurred, 'it's not like there's anyone here but us.'

There came a loud crashing noise from the farthest corner.

'I'm cursed,' Len muttered, throwing his empty beer can towards where the noise had come from.

Sidecar was already on her feet and running at the barrier. She started pounding on it with her fists, shouting at the top of her lungs for Molly to let them out.

'Shut up for God's sake,' Molly shouted, 'can't hear myself think. I'll have to go and fetch someone. I can't see how you get it open from out here.'

'Quickly!' Sidecar begged. 'There's something in here with us!'

'Yeah...' Molly muttered. 'Derek's B.O.' She jogged towards the exit.

'What was it, do you think?' Roll-Up asked, backing away from the table towards the light of the fridges.

'How am I supposed to know?' Beef replied, pulling Len after him. 'Derek! Come on!'

Derek stayed sat down. 'Tentacles,' he muttered.

'Yeah, mate, tentacles...' Len replied, 'just what I was thinking.'

'Get over here, Derek!' Roll-Up shouted.

'Tentacles,' Derek replied before getting calmly to his feet and picking up the chair he was sitting on. There was the sound of something moving amongst the overturned tables and chairs. Metal chair legs scraped against the polished floor as whatever had collided with the furniture made some space. Derek pointed the chair, legs-first, towards where the noise was coming from. 'Tentacles,' he said again before running into the darkness with a roar, stabbing the chair in front of him.

'Derek!' Roll-Up shouted, as Beef dragged Len towards the Barrier. Derek's roar cut off with a high-pitched squeal followed by a wet, popping sound.

'Derek?' Roll-Up asked.

Beef screamed as a round object flew past his face, bouncing off the metal shutters and rolling along the floor. It came to a lopsided halt at the foot of one of the drinks fridges. It was Derek's head. He wasn't even *remotely* glamorous anymore.

Chapter Thirteen

HOWARD HAD HEARD Hubcap banging his way back up to the third floor for a few minutes and was in the hallway by the time he came crashing through the fire-doors.

'Knew you were coming, didn't I?' he said. 'Used my mystic powers.'

'You trying to wind me up?' Hubcap asked, trying to get his breath back.

'A bit,' Howard nodded. 'Hoped it might stop you wanting to smack me.'

'Still think you and I need to walk into the city?'

'Yep.'

'Then I still want to smack you. It can wait for now though, we've a bit of an emergency on our hands.'

'I know,' Howard gave an awkward, half-smile. 'There's a horrible monster-thing outside that's killed Jerry and Sally.'

'You heard me telling people on the way up?'

Howard shook his head. 'Considering you were the one that made such a fuss on the way here about how weird stuff happens all the time, I wish you'd be a bit more open minded.'

Hubcap made to reply, but growled and bit back whatever he had been about to say. 'Alright. I'll hear you out, but we walk at the same time.'

'No problem.' They headed back toward the stairs. 'It was like… this sounds stupid… I was remembering stuff that hasn't actually happened yet.'

'Yeah, it does sound stupid.'

'But no more stupid than killer pigeons.'

Hubcap actually smiled slightly. 'Guess not.'

'Maybe I'm just imagining it, tapped in the head…'

'Yeah, maybe.'

'Thing is, there *is* a way to find out.'

'Oh yeah?'

'Yeah… so, if it turns out I *am* right and not just a nutter you met on the road, will you come with me?'

Hubcap laughed, 'We having a bet now?'

'If you like.'

Hubcap stuck his hand out. 'If you can prove to me that you can somehow see the future—I mean really *prove* it, mind—I'll go with you, OK?'

Howard shook his hand. 'OK.'

They started to descend the stairs.

'Well?' Hubcap shouted, his voice echoing up the stairwell. 'Go on then!'

'Remember the name Adrian.'

'What?'

'Do you know a song called "Shake Out?"' Hubcap rolled his eyes, '"Shake out, break out, come over here let's make out", that ear turd by Fadz?'

'No idea…' Hubcap started to sing it and Howard grinned. 'That's it.'

'What about it?' Hubcap asked.

'Remember that too.'

Hubcap couldn't help but laugh. 'I am *so* going to smack you…'

Chapter Fourteen

It HAD NOT expected the ceiling to be so fragile, so little seemed to be able to take its weight these days

It flopped around until it found its balance, chattering some of its teeth in its eagerness.

Some of the meat started screaming, which made its nerves jangle. It turned its deaf ears towards the noise, but it didn't much help.

The meat was accelerating towards it! This put another familiar flavour in its brain. Pleasure? Jealousy? Not sure, it always got those two mixed up.

The meat was trying to attack it with a chair. This was good, aggression gave the bone marrow a little extra fizz. It flung the chair away, grabbed the meat and made it shush by pulling off the noisy bit. There was nothing it needed from that, so it threw the head at the others. While it sucked on the hot fountain of the meat's neck, its fingers probed the body to see what was what. It slit, poked and unravelled, laying out the components for study. The thigh muscles were impressive and it craved them for its own; the biceps too were fat, like peeled watermelons.

It poked the trimmings into its mouths (floppy offal and redundant pipes) and began to strip and prepare the components it liked.

The rest of the meat was screaming very loudly now, but it managed to blank that out, concentrating on the job in hand. Even without rushing—for the sake of aching stomachs—it managed to strip and process the meat in just under a minute. As much as it enjoyed bringing an element of play to the dining table, it chose to run economically now, laying itself flat on the floor and reaching out to snatch the rest of them.

It could hear the sound of more cattle outside. This was normal, they were drawn by the slaughterhouse choir like all animals. A little game occurred to it that might be both amusing and nourishing...

Chapter Fifteen

SIDECAR WAS BABBLING now. After the shock of Derek's head rebounding off the shutter in front of her she had given up on all attempts at reasoned communication, now she was just making noise.

Beef wasn't much better and certainly when he felt something grab at his ankles he wailed as loudly as everyone else. Roll-Up gave the creature a fight, hacking at the limbs with the back of a chair. It gained him all of four or five extra seconds which wasn't enough, even though rescue was on its way as Little Chef and a gang of bikers were heading through the main door towards them.

Len was the only one to go quietly, toppling backwards into the shadows and sliding from sight with nothing but the squeak of his rubber heels on the floor tiles.

Little Chef drew to a halt outside the metal door, holding his arms out to either side so as to stop the rest of them.

'We can't hang about!' Val shouted, 'they must be hurt in there.'

'Screams like that and the mess we saw outside? They're more than *hurt*, Val, and you know it.'

Little Chef started heading forward through the shadowy hall. The lights from the vending machines bounced excitedly off the beige walls. Some of the games were auto-playing, demonstrating how fun they were with volleys of machine-gun fire and the roar of Formula One engines. Over the noise Little Chef could hear the security shutters rattling in their frame as they began to open. From the dark of the restaurant, a single figure stumbled out into the half-light of the hall. It was Sidecar. She stretched her fat arms towards them and Little Chef could tell that they were wet, the reds and greens of the arcade games glistening off them like gang colours.

'What's happening, Sidecar?' he asked.

'For God's sake!' Val pushed past him. 'You can see she's not right.'

'Val!' Little Chef hissed. 'Get back here.'

She ignored him, determined to offer help. As she drew close to Sidecar though she began to wonder if she shouldn't have listened to him.

'Sidecar?' she asked, disturbed by the way the woman's head lolled to one side. As she stepped closer, the lights caught Sidecar's face and Val bit her lip at the sight of the slack mouth and the gashes that ran from cheek to cheek. The body of Sidecar was held by the creature inside the restaurant. It played the corpse like a puppet, its fingers twanging on the dead nerve-endings as deftly as those of a guitar player. The body reared up at the creature's command and grabbed hold of the now screaming Val, yanking her back into the restaurant.

Little Chef's eyes were getting used to the darkness. As the creature moved, he saw enough to get a sense of how big the thing was. It made him rethink his plans.

'Get back!' he shouted to those behind him, just as the bodies of Roll-Up, Beef and Len emerged into the hallway. They hovered on the end of the thick limbs that held them, their feet barely skimming the ground as the root in their backs took the weight. Little Chef ran towards the entrance, waving at everyone to get out of the building. Behind him the corpses swayed and gave pursuit, their lifeless arms stretching out to grab him as they floated through the air. He jumped through the decorative display of plastic plants in the middle of the hallway, a spray of artificial leaves scattering around him as he ducked below Beef's heavy legs. He rolled to one side as Roll-Up landed like a splayed crab, his wiry arms and legs grabbing at him like the mechanised claw that attempted to snatch teddy-bears in the arcade area. Little Chef was back on his feet and running towards the entrance before Roll-Up's spindly fingers could grab him.

'Get ready to close the doors!' he shouted. The rest of the group were already on the other side of the glass. He had no idea how successful the sliding panels would be at keeping the thing inside, they weren't built to be that secure.

He ran through the opening, his momentum carrying him straight into Tank who grabbed him to stop him falling.

Someone operated the manual control that locked the doors together and everybody stepped back as the three dead bikers pressed themselves against the thick glass.

Beef was in the middle, his large face distorted against the glass. His fat tongue rolled like a slug in a trail of its own spit.

'We need to block this off properly.' Little Chef said, waving away the questions people were asking him until he had time in which to answer them.

'Tiger's on it.' Tank replied. There was the sound of a heavy truck engine firing up and a pair of headlights flooded the car park.

Tiger swung the long-haul truck in a wide arc and began to circle around so as to drive past the front of the building.

Roll-Up's nails beat a drum rhythm on the glass. Beef began head-butting the door. Len swung his heavy boots at the glass over and over again. There was a cracking noise.

'He's not going to get here in time.' Little Chef muttered, pushing everyone back from the door.

Chapter Sixteen

'HE'S NOT GOING to get there in time.' Howard said as he and Hubcap stepped out of the motel and looked across at the gathered crowd in front of the main building.

'Who isn't?' asked Hubcap.

Howard shook his head, trying to hold on to the brief images he'd seen and get as much information from them as he could.

A thought occurred to him. 'Can you drive a motorbike?'

'Like a demon.' Hubcap replied without a pause.

'Seriously?'

'Of course "seriously". Tank taught me when I first got here.'

'Come on then.' Howard set off at a run.

They could hear shouting from the crowd, but weren't to know until later it was in response to Val being snatched.

Howard ran onto the grass by the petrol station where several large motorbikes were parked. 'Take your pick,' he said.

'Seriously?'

'Of course "seriously",' Howard replied, mimicking Hubcap. 'Be quick, we haven't got long.'

'Long before what?' Hubcap asked eyeing up the bikes and pulling a length of wire from his jacket pocket.

'Before that creature—whatever it is—comes bursting out of there and starts killing everybody.'

'Oh yeah,' Hubcap smiled, '*that*.' He picked a bike and was about to force the wire into the ignition when he stopped. 'Seriously, Little Chef's going to kill me if we do this.'

'No he won't' Howard promised, 'he'll think you're wonderful, now *please*, get on with it.'

Hubcap sighed. 'Alright. You're just lucky that riding a bike wasn't the only thing Tank taught me how to do.'

They heard Tank start the lorry up.

'Quickly!' Howard shouted.

The motorbike turned over with a roar.

'Hop on!' said Hubcap.

Chapter Seventeen

'HA'S NOT GOING to get here in time.'

The door cracked right down the middle where Beef was pounding at it, his head poking out in a spider-web of shattered glass.

Little Chef pulled a knife out of his back pocket.

Tank was preparing to swing a length of chain he was holding. 'This is going to get nasty,' he said, his eyes darting to where Tiger was still turning the lorry to come alongside the doorway.

The door shattered and Beef's body came thrusting out, snatching with its arms and legs.

'Keep back!' Little Chef shouted, though he needn't have worried, everyone was falling over themselves to stay out of reach.

The first anyone knew of Howard and Hubcap was the high-pitched whine of the bike engine, closely followed by the sound of Hubcap wailing in panic.

They came from the opposite direction to Tiger, Hubcap doing his best not to crash, but scarcely able to believe they were still moving (Tank had only ever let him drive around the car park and never at more than 30 miles per hour). On the back, Howard was gripping the seat as tightly as he could with his legs, leaving his hands free to aim the jousting lance they had taken from next to the bike. The thing that had once been Beef turned towards the noise and the lance hit it square in its belly. The impact shoved Howard off the back of the bike. He let go of the lance and rolled along the forecourt away from the creature's flailing arms. Hubcap kept going for a second longer, hitting the brakes as hard as he could, before the bike toppled over and he too fell to the ground.

Beef's body was yanked backwards through the shattered doorway just as you would snatch a burned finger away from a flame.

Tiger swerved to avoid Hubcap as he lined the cab up with the doorway. He took the best aim he could before letting go of the wheel and bracing himself for the impact. The lorry smashed out the rest of the glass doors and wedged itself, sideways on, in the opening. After a few seconds, the passenger door swung open and Tiger appeared with a wide grin on his face.

'And... we're parked,' he chuckled, lowering himself to the ground.

Howard got to his feet and ran towards Hubcap who was groaning loudly.

'You alright?' Howard asked, dropping to his haunches beside his friend. 'You break anything?'

'"Drive at it" he says.' Hubcap moaned. 'Have you still got that lance thing? I want to put it into you... find it for me... let it be my dying wish.'

'You're mad!' Little Chef laughed, running towards them. 'The pair of you!' He patted Howard hard enough on the back to knock him off balance, then dropped down to Hubcap. 'You OK?' he asked, still laughing. 'Don't spoil it by being a big girl now.'

'I hate you.' Hubcap muttered. 'I've probably snapped my spine and you're all congratulating me.'

'*Have* you snapped your spine?' Little Chef asked.

'No.'

'Then get up, we've got to figure out what we're going to do next.'

He turned to the rest of the remaining citizens of the Kingdom of Welcome Break. 'Change of plan,' he said, 'that thing has taken the main building, and I suggest we let it keep it for now. When it's light and we see what we're facing, then maybe that can change. For now I don't intend to lose another person to it. Agreed?'

There was a mumble of agreement.

'Good. We're going to stay right here, out in the open. I want a team of people on fire duty, we're going to get cold without one. I also need people to get to the stores and get these lamps lit. We've been conserving supplies by removing most of the street-lighting, not anymore, now I want the place to *glow*. I don't want a single shadow left where the thing can hide.' He looked to Tiger. 'Sort out a roster of guys to keep an eye on all the exits; we need to know the minute it tries to move.' Tiger nodded and moved off to get some of his boys together.

'Right,' Little Chef sighed, 'other than that, we watch each other's backs and make damn sure every single one of us makes it through to dawn.'

Chapter Eighteen

HUBCAP AND HOWARD joined the team sent to the stores. Hubcap had wanted to build the fire but nobody seemed to think that was a good idea.

'Light bulbs,' he moaned as they walked around the back of the main building towards the set of Portakabins that were used for storage. 'We save the day in an act of almost *unbelievable* coolness, and the reward is light bulb duty. I hate my life.'

'Better than smashing up stuff to build a fire. That's hard work.'

'You see, now, I *like* smashing stuff, I'm good at it.' Hubcap winked. 'I am working against my specific skill set here.'

'"Skill set"?' Howard rolled his eyes. 'Where did you pick that up from?'

'Dad,' Hubcap admitted, 'he always spoke like that.'

'Sorry,' Howard felt awkward, 'I didn't mean to…'

'Shut up,' Hubcap said playfully. 'It's too much like hard work if you're going to get all embarrassed every time my dad gets mentioned. He's dead, yeah... doesn't mean he didn't sound like an arse sometimes,' he smiled. 'Mind you... if *you* said that I'd knock your teeth out.'

'Good to know.'

'Yeah, you might want to note it down in that book of yours, "The various reasons the noble Hubcap will clean my teeth for me using his knuckles... reason number one: bad-mouthing his father."'

'Noted.'

'"Reason number two: talking mystical toss and being all, y'know... *ooooh*..."' Hubcap waved his fingers at Howard.

'Ok, see my previous answers on this subject.'

'Fair enough. "Reason number three..."' Hubcap thought for a moment. 'Well, we'll come back to reason number three, but I suspect it'll have something to do with puddings. As you know I feel very strongly about puddings.'

'How many of us does it take to fetch some light bulbs anyway?' said Howard. Leading the group was one of the oldest bikers Howard had seen since he had arrived. Snakebite (who knew how he got such a cool name? It certainly didn't suit him) had long white hair and a rolling walk that spoke of years with a bike between the thighs. There was also a woman called Vanessa that Howard was doing his best to avoid. She seemed permanently angry, the sort of person that would happily pop you one just for being within reach. Another guy, Fritz, turned out to be American which—considering his name—confused Howard no end.

'Is that a joke?' Hubcap asked. '"How many post-apocalyptic biker dudes does it take to fetch a light bulb?"'

'I don't now, how many?'

'Five apparently.'

'Hilarious.'

'Welcome to my life.'

'Stand back!' Snakebite shouted as they reached the Portakabin. 'Who knows what might be in here?'

'Homicidal earwigs?' Hubcap whispered.

'Psycho spiders?' Howard replied.

'Are they armed?'

'Oh yes! *Heavily*.'

Hubcap smirked and Snakebite gave him a dirty look. 'You'll be laughing on the other side of your face when you're being torn to pieces by some 'orrible creature!'

'I *so* won't.' Hubcap replied, straight-faced.

'Where is the other side of your face?' Howard wondered aloud. Hubcap gave his arm a slap. 'Ah! Don't do that, I have just fallen off a motorbike you know, I have bruises.'

'He's very delicate,' Hubcap said to the others. 'Goes by the name of Howard.'

Fritz laughed, nobody else did.

'Sorry,' Hubcap said, 'carry on.'

The old man opened the door and jumped back out of

the way. For a few moments absolutely nothing happened. Then, nothing happened a bit more.

'Right,' said Hubcap walking past everybody and into the store, 'shall we get the bulbs then, or what?'

Chapter Nineteen

THE CREATURE SPAT on the shiny side of the chiller cabinet and polished the metal with the heel of one of its hands. Angling the surface to the light, it studied its own reflection. Beef had owned a strong face, firm jaw, powerful forehead. It didn't look the same second-hand. Peeling off the borrowed skin, it reached for Sidecar's face and tried that instead. Sidecar had been screaming when it had taken the face, no amount of easing and teasing with its fingers seemed to hide the fact. The mouth just hung slack. It whipped it off and flung it to the far corner of the restaurant where it hit the floor with the sound of wet swimming trunks thrown against the tiled wall of a changing room.

It was fast running out of entertainment.

The pain caused when the little meat had stabbed one of its puppets had long since passed. The anger had not. It was not used to being hurt. It had not known that it was so *sensitive* to pain caused in its appendages. It was something it must be careful not to allow again.

A shiver rippled through its stomachs and it tried to decide whether it was indigestion or a plan. Eventually it decided on the latter as a number of images describing something new passed through its brain. Oh yes, this was good... all it needed was meat and motor parts. It began to tear apart the kitchen equipment.

Chapter Twenty

THE FIRE WAS quick to build. Nobody had felt precious about the preservation of furniture and a chain of people had passed along chairs and writing desks from the empty motel rooms.

By the time the lighting party returned, the fire was spluttering with new flames. Between them, they carried two boxes of what Vanessa insisted were 'Sodium Vapour Tubes'. Howard and Hubcap mutually agreed these were still to be thought of as 'light bulbs' because neither of them wanted to sound like a geek. They were also carrying two extendible ladders in order to be able to reach the lamps.

When Little Chef saw them, he ran over and they split into two teams, the better to get the job done quickly.

'We'll sort those closest to the buildings first,' Little Chef said, 'then spread out from there.'

The two teams started almost next to one another. Vanessa shimmied up one ladder and Fritz took the other. The tubes in place, they moved apart taking the next lamp in turn. Howard went with Fritz, holding the ladder for him while he replaced the tubes.

'So,' asked Howard, 'you don't sound very German.'

'Huh?' Fritz looked baffled for a second before the penny dropped. 'Oh… the name. No, it's just a nickname, my real name's 'Joe' but I used to be a repairman. You know: you called me if something was "on the fritz". Broken. You never hear that expression?'

'No.' *More to the point,* Howard thought. *If you were a repairman why give yourself a nickname that meant "broken"?*

'Must be an American thing.'

'Maybe.' Howard changed the subject. "Were you over here when it happened then?'

'The Change? Yeah… My brother lived here, I was visiting. Nobody really crosses the oceans anymore, too many people say they've seen… *things* in them.'

'I read about that.'

'Yeah… I heard you don't remember any of it?'

'That's right.'

Fritz nodded. 'People talk. This stuff was worldwide kid. The things themselves, in the sky, there was a video of that online but it soon got pulled, drove people mad even seeing it second-hand. Then the stuff that came after. When the TV still worked, the news showed everything. They had footage of dead Sioux taking the White House. Native Indian *skeletons*, skulls wearing feather headdresses and war-paint, the full thing y'know? All riding up the lawn on horses, taking out the suits in security with bows and arrows. Japan had dinosaurs for God's sake... chewing up skyscrapers and fighting one another in the middle of Tokyo. Nowhere's any better than here.'

'Have you been into London?'

'Since it happened? Yeah, right at the beginning. I was still with Tony then, my brother. He'd been seeing this girl... worked nights as a nurse in the city. When it happened, she was still on shift and he was terrified. The mobile network went down... *everything* went down... there was no way of knowing if she was ok. He wanted to mount some kind of rescue mission, drive in there and get her out. It took the government a while to get their act together, getting the military out, cordoning off the roads and stuff. We got some way before we started hitting road blocks, but in the end it was obvious we were going to have to try and get through on foot. Tony didn't get far.' Fritz paused in what he was doing. 'The army shot him trying to cross Blackfriars Bridge.'

'They shot him?'

'Yeah.' Fritz locked the tube into position and began to replace the casing. 'You've got to realise everybody was freaking out, the army was no different. They just had guns. Martial law lasted for about a week, maybe ten days. Then the world stopped pretending to be in control of itself and it was every man for himself.' Fritz slid down the ladder, his feet gripping the outside of the rungs. 'Things were crazy for a long time before people started to work together again.'

'Have you met other groups like this?' asked Howard.

'Yeah, a couple.' They began to move along to the next lamp. 'There was a bunch of ladies working out of Welwyn Garden City that I fell foul of,' Fritz grinned. 'They decided that it was all men's fault and were hanging any they found.'

'I'll avoid that then,' said Howard.

'There was a cool group over Ealing way though. Bit too... I don't know... *vegetarian* for me,' he shrugged. 'All very "peace brother" and hippy. Not my thing. Nice enough though.' They propped the ladder against the new lamp. 'To be honest I find it kinda hard to fit in with most groups, this is the first crowd I think I've actually enjoyed being a part of since I was at High School.'

Howard nodded. 'Let's hope it's still here come tomorrow then.'

'It will be... or it won't.' Fritz started to climb the ladder. 'People are different these days. You get used to stuff. I mean, six months ago, if I'd seen something like that thing in there... well, I wouldn't still be stood here. We've seen so much though, so many impossible things in so short a time. You get almost numb to it. Not that it doesn't scare you, or that you don't care when you see a good pal get himself killed but... I don't know, I guess you just learn to function with it all. People die, it's sad, but we've all lost so many we just can't afford to let it slow us up. We just do what we do best: get on with it.'

Chapter Twenty-One

HUBCAP WAS ON the opposite side of the car-park from Howard holding Vanessa's ladder and keeping his head down (in case she decided to bite it off).

'Moody cow isn't she?' Little Chef whispered in his ear. 'Knows her stuff though.'

'I heard that, short arse!' Vanessa shouted from above them.

Little Chef pulled a face and winked at Hubcap. 'How's the new kid then?'

Hubcap shrugged. 'He's ok.'

'What? You had a falling out already? He's only been here five minutes!'

'Nah… it's not that. He's just, kind of weird.'

'Aren't we all?'

'Yeah, but…' Hubcap sighed. 'You know he doesn't remember anything, right? Val told you about that?'

'Yeah.'

'Well, he thinks he knows stuff that's *going* to happen instead of stuff that already has.'

'Like what?'

'Just bits of stuff. He knew that creature was going to burst out of the door before Tiger got there.'

'*I* could have told you that.'

'No, he actually said it when you were still *inside*. That's how come we had time to nick the bike and everything.'

'OK, that's more impressive. What else has he said?'

'Some weird stuff about someone called Adrian…'

'I used to know a guy called Adrian. He was my boss when I worked haulage.'

'Probably not the same Adrian.'

'Probably not. Did he mention a wart?'

'No.'

'Definitely not the same guy, you couldn't mention my Adrian without bringing up the wart. Thing was like a hairy cricket ball.'

'Stop gassing and get the ladder shifted,' Vanessa shouted, stomping down past them and marching on to the next lamp. Little Chef sighed, grabbed the base of the ladder and walked after her. Hubcap caught the other end and followed on.

'Can I keep talking?' Hubcap asked her, once they'd set the ladder up again and Vanessa was at work.

'Of course.'

'He wants me to go with him into London.'

'What for?' asked Little Chef.

'He doesn't know. Just says he has to go; like it's his mission in life or something.'

'You want to go?'

'You kidding? It was all I could do before to get *out* of there.'

'Yeah, must admit it would take a lot to see me heading in that direction too.' Little Chef glanced up, Vanessa was hammering at the lamp casing in anger as the screws were refusing to turn. 'Where's he got the idea from?''I don't know, just popped into his head, I think. It was after that stuff during the magic act.'

'Good act, tentacles... who knew they could pull that off?'

'Erm...' Hubcap squirmed a little. 'I kind of think that *wasn't* part of the trick.'

'I was joking.' Little Chef smiled at him.

'Oh... yeah. Well, it was after that. When he came round he was full of all this "got to go to London...it's my destiny" stuff.'

'Being fried by a gadget with all the sophistication of a coat hanger and then knocked out by a tentacle will do weird things to you.'

'I guess.'

'The question, of course, is: what if he's right?'

'Eh?'

'What if he actually *can* see the future, really *does* need to walk into the city, and you really *should* go with him.'

'Well... erm... when you put it like that...'

'Come on!' Vanessa said, jumping to the floor between them and marching off with her toolbox in hand.

'Worth thinking about though isn't it?' Little Chef said, grabbing the ladder again.

Hubcap grabbed his end and walked in silence for a moment before a thought occurred to him, 'Oi! Are you just trying to get rid of me?'

Chapter Twenty-Two

LLOYD WAS FINDING this hard. Being on Tiger's crew meant you accepted a degree of danger, knew you were going to be sticking your neck out from time-to-time. Still, tonight was different. He'd been on the front row as Beef—or whatever was left of him—had smashed his way through the glass doors of the main building and it had scared him stupid. Not that he would tell anyone that of course, none of them were the sort of men to own up to feelings like that. They were friends, yes. Friends that went out on their bikes and spent just as much time getting drunk and smashing stuff up as they did hunting for food and equipment. They were not the sort of men that sat down and talked about their deepest feelings and insecurities. Still, whether he would admit it or not, Lloyd was terrified.

Tiger had dotted the members of the crews in pairs around the buildings. While those stationed at the front had an increasing amount of light, those at the back were having to make do with their torches. Lloyd could see the torchlight of both couples on either side him. It didn't make him feel any better.

'What are you doing back there Gary?' he shouted.

'You know what I'm doing,' came a voice from behind a large rubbish dumpster, 'you don't want a running commentary do you?'

'I want to know I've got back-up in case something kicks off.' 'You will,' Gary replied, 'in a *minute.*'

'Should have gone before you came,' Lloyd muttered, 'or held onto it.'

'If I'd held onto this beast, pal, I'd have split in half. Don't know what's wrong with me, must have been that All Day Breakfast stuff.'

'I really don't need to know this.' Lloyd groaned.

'Look on the bright side,' Gary continued with a chuckle. 'If that thing comes our way at least we'll have something big to hit it with!'

Lloyd groaned. 'Just get on with it will you?'

'Nearly there.'

There was a screeching noise, like splitting wood.

'Gary?'

'Wasn't me! My guts aren't *that* bad.'

Lloyd shone his torch along the wall in front of him. 'Can't see anything.'

The windows, safety glass blackened by the emissions of exhaust pipes, were intact. There was a fire exit a few metres away, it was firmly closed. The creaking noise came again.

'Seriously,' Gary shouted, 'what *is* that?'

'Finish up and help me find out.'

Gary stepped out from behind the dumpster, pulling his belt tight. 'I was all done the moment I heard that noise, pal. Like a torpedo it was.' Gary added his own torch beam to Lloyd's. 'It definitely came from close...' The light of his torch fell on a small air vent to their right. It was just above head height and had once been sealed with a slatted wooden cover. The cover was now missing.

'That huge thing couldn't fit through there,' Lloyd said. 'Little Chef said it took up half the restaurant.'

'Well *something* must have come out of there,' Gary replied.

'We should shout for the others.' Lloyd turned towards the bobbing torchlight to his left.

There was a hissing and slapping noise and something small moved towards them from the shadows of the wall.

'Guys!' Lloyd shouted to the others, shining his torch towards the noise. Gary did the same, both of them stepping backwards as they took in what was coming at them.

There was certainly some of Roll-Up in there. His yellow face was stretched wide across a metal frame made from bent spoons. There was nothing behind the face and the harsh light of the torches lit up the veins and capillaries in his skin. Below the 'neck' was a whirling mess of muscles and the motor from an industrial food blender. As the thing moved forward, the meat hissed and cooked against the exposed machinery. It smelt like pork on a barbecue.

'That's so sick,' Gary said, looking across to the other bikers in the distance. 'Get over here! You've got to see this thing it's...'

The machine unfolded itself. Two 'wings' made from the serrated blades of bread knives swung out from behind its back and cut into Gary's leg. He shouted and fell forwards, sticking his hands out to defend himself. Flapping the mouth of its trap, the machine took away his fingers. Lloyd swung the cricket bat he was holding and knocked it away before it could do any more damage. It rolled into the darkness as the other bikers appeared, everyone shining their torches after it while Gary lay screaming on the floor.

'Shut up, Gary!' Lloyd hissed, hearing other noises in the dark.

'My fingers!' Gary squealed between clenched teeth. One of the others, a young guy called Danny, had a bit of medical training and was quick to bind his belt around Gary's arm to try and stop the bleeding. The leg was even worse, his jeans thick with blood.

'There's something else out here,' Lloyd said. 'Any of you hear that?'

As well as the motor that powered what was left of Roll-Up, they could hear a new noise, a high-pitched whine, almost a buzzing. There was a sudden whistling noise as something flew past them in the dark. All of them flung their torch beams in all directions, trying to catch a glimpse of whatever it was circling above them.

'Did you see that?' one of them said 'Anyone?'

'Nah... too quick,' another replied.

The noise came again and Lloyd actually caught it in his torch as it shot past his left ear and, with a flash of metal, opened the throat of the guy stood beside him.

"Oh my god...' Lloyd whispered as the other man dropped to his knees, gargling and bleeding out on to the ground.

It had flown on thin, chrome wings, its body a glistening bulb of thigh muscle. Sidecar's blonde hair had streamed behind what Lloyd could only assume were her now-detached eyeballs. A beard of rotating cutlery buzzed in front of the creature, providing both a degree of lift and sufficient weaponry to ensure it was lethal.

Lloyd began screaming for help.

Chapter Twenty-Three

LLOYD'S SCREAMS CUT through the cheer that had erupted in appreciation of the new lights. The bonfire was in full swing and people had dared to think they might survive the night.

Tiger had returned to the front of the building but wasted no time in waving his men towards the noise and leading a crew to the rescue.

Little Chef was also quick to respond. 'Everyone keep together!' he shouted. 'This is good, this is what we want. Whatever that thing is it must be trying to escape. We've got it on the run!'

He even got the crowd to give a little cheer at that as he led the rest of Tiger's crews round the back.

'No.' Howard whispered to himself, though Hubcap certainly heard him. 'That's not what's happening at all.'

Chapter Twenty-Four

'WHAT'S HAPPENING?' TANK shouted as he ran towards the crew that had been guarding the rear. They had gathered in one place, forming a rough circle and keeping the beams of their torches on the move. The man with the cut throat was dead and nobody wished to join him. Garry was lifted onto two men's shoulders and ferried away.

A heavily muscled guy with a razored-smooth head and a tattoo that earned him the name Python held a baseball bat high as he inched towards the incoming reinforcements. 'They're not big,' he said as Tank drew close, Tiger and the rest of the crew just behind him. 'But…'

There was a deep-throated roar and a shape danced through torch beams as it sped along the ground towards the gathered men. This didn't show as many body parts as the other creations, appearing little more than a rectangular box on wheels.

'What's that?' Tiger asked. 'A remote-controlled car or something?'

'This one's new,' Python replied.

The box exploded, showering everyone in metal shrapnel, pieces of saucepans, mixing bowls; all broken-up, sharp and happy to cut when hurled fast enough.

Tiger was lucky, he got his hand up quick enough that a teaspoon handle stabbed into his palm rather than face. Tank too avoided all but a gash to the cheek. Some others were not so lucky, none of the wounds were enough to kill but there was panic and screams of pain as the remains of Sidecar swooped down again, her metal beard adding to the carnage.

A new noise joined the mix: a bubbling, hissing sound. A five foot metal canister appeared, wreathed in a thick cloak of steam. Propelled by a rudimentary caterpillar track, it was slow but that didn't reassure anybody. The front of the tube held the face of Liquid Len, grotesquely stretched around the cone of a funnel, his open mouth the source of the steam.

'Keep back!' Little Chef shouted, having arrived in time to guess exactly what was about to happen.

'Cover yourselves!' Tank added, sharing Little Chef's fears.

The machine began to spray boiling hot water from Len's mouth. Those who could, turned their faces away from the scalding jet. Others were not so lucky.

Little Chef grabbed his leather riding gloves from his belt and pulled them on as he ran toward the machine. Avoiding the spray, he jumped at the cylinder, giving a pained shout as the hot metal singed his cheek. He grabbed the top edge and used his weight to turn the thing away from the bikers. He heard the buzz of the flying creature, no doubt intending to cut him down.

It scythed towards him, metal beard whining at high-speed. As it came down to head level, Tank jumped at it with a roar, swinging his chain at its body and knocking it from the air.

'I hate flying, biting things!' he shouted, bringing the chain down again and again. The buzzing pulsed as it tried to regain the air. Tank wouldn't let it. 'Stop... your... *noise*!' he shouted, lashing at it with every word. Eventually, it did.

The steaming water-urn toppled over and Little Chef rolled out of the way as its contents poured out.

'Fancy a cup of tea?' Tiger asked, helping him up.

'I'd prefer something stronger,' Little Chef replied.

Tank walked over to them, his chain hanging loose from his hand. 'One left lads.'

'Yep.' Tiger shone his torch at the Roll-Up machine.

Little Chef picked up a length of metal pipe from where one of the other bikers had dropped it. 'On three?'

'Aye...' Tank replied. 'One...'

'Two...' said Tiger.

Little Chef gripped the pipe tightly. 'Three!'

They attacked.

Chapter Twenty-Five

'TOTALLY MISSING THE point,' Howard muttered, shaking his head and desperately trying to pin down the images from his "dream". 'It wasn't an escape attempt…'

'What is it?' Hubcap asked, coming to stand next to him.

Howard shook his head again. 'Can't remember… but it wasn't an escape attempt…'

Hubcap looked towards the lorry that was keeping the creature in, did he just see it move?

'Think,' he said. 'What was it?'

Howard suddenly tensed, the images falling into place. 'A distraction,' he whispered.

The lorry shook and the air was filled with the sound of grinding metal. It moved towards them as it was pushed from the other side. It began to rise, as the creature lifted and then hurled the lorry towards the crowd. The cab twisted in the air as if turning to look at the people scattering before it. It hit the fire in a spray of sparks and a squeal of metal. People ran, screaming in fear or pain, as hot embers rained down on their fleeing heads.

In the doorway, now fully lit by the street-lamps, the creature took it all in. It was a grotesque of flesh and metal, a soup of bodies and cars. That first night that Howard had heard it he had assumed it had been *riding* some sort of vehicle. This had been a mistake. The thrusting pistons and spinning gears were part of its body, cannibalised from abandoned vehicles. They pumped and turned, more capable of propelling the huge mass of the creature than its original legs, which were lost in the cluster of limbs that rippled from its flattened-out hips. At first glance, its arms appeared overly long and bizarrely jointed. Looking closer, it became clear that each arm was made up of many, stitched end to end, elbow to palm. If it had too many arms, what was to be said of its heads? They lined its chest like a necklace of pearls, featureless for the most part, nothing but vessels for the wide, constantly snapping mouths. Its main head was a bulbous thing, tumorous lumps robbing it of its shape. Thick trails of motor oil ran from its eyes.

There was a loud hiss as the hydraulics lodged in its abdomen projected it from the doorway to the car park in one leap. It's ridiculously elongated arms flailed as it sailed through the air. A jet of steam erupted from a pipe in its spine, releasing the pressure of its internal engine. Both muscles and springs creaked as it found its balance. It reached out a number of its long, long arms and snatched some of the bikers that had been felled either by lorry or fire. Howard watched as it took them apart. One mouth extinguished some flaming hair like puffing out a candle. Fingers probed and unravelled the bodies like a man shelling peanuts, before dropping the wet bits it didn't intend to reuse into its various mouths. It seemed to show no enthusiasm for the task, its face slack, a string of saliva dangling from the corner of its mouth, a gold chain, glistening in the reflection of the fires.

'We need to draw its attention.' Howard said.

'Oh sod off!' Hubcap shouted. 'Are you an absolute mentalist or what?!' All of Hubcap's built-up tension chose that moment to snap. 'First of all, you tell me I have to come with you to London, then, you tell me I have to drive at that thing on a motorbike. Now, you want me to draw its attention. Seriously... how much must you absolutely *hate* me? If you're so desperate to see me killed why don't you just whack me over the head with a brick or something? Eh? *Eh?*' Hubcap was shouting at the top of his voice now, getting more and more angry as Howard refused to react, just staring over his shoulder. 'The last thing I want is that thing after me... you hear? Eh? *Are you even bloody listening?*'

Howard snapped out of it. 'Hm? No... I wasn't, to be honest. *It* was though, well done.'

Hubcap turned around to see the monster staring at him, thoughts of the other humans gone from its mind for now.

'I hate my life,' Hubcap sighed. 'Have I mentioned that before?'

He turned on his heels and began to run as fast as he could.

'Wait!' Howard shouted, chasing after him. 'You can't outrun it! All you'll do is make it attack you quicker...'

There was the sound of pulsing hydraulics which could only mean it was jumping after them.

Hubcap gritted his teeth and tried to go even faster. Howard looked up, watching for where it was going to land.

There was a crash as it hit the canopy of the petrol station just ahead of them. The metal and neon buckled and popped beneath the creature's weight and the whole structure collapsed, the roof shearing off a couple of the pump machines. The creature roared, trying to keep its balance as everything crumpled around it.

'Please tell me those pumps are empty,' Howard said.

'You kidding?' Hubcap replied. 'With this many bikers? It's one of the main things Tiger's crews hunt for on The Perimeter. We have three or four full tanker lorries that keep it serviced.'

'That's really not a good thing for it to be doing then,' Howard replied, watching as the creature pounded on the canopy, lifting and tearing the metal, flinging it away in fury.

Suddenly it caught sight of the boys again and the

irritation of the collapsing petrol station was forgotten. It shot out an arm to grab them. Hubcap rolled on the ground trying to avoid the fingers and was devastated to see Howard doing the opposite. It looked like Howard *wanted* to be caught; jumping around, throwing himself between the snatching hands and Hubcap.

'Do the song!' Howard shouted as the creature got a firm hold on him.

'What?' Hubcap shouted.

'You know! The song I told you to remember! Sing it!'

'You have *got* to be joking…'

'Of course I'm not bloody joking! It's going to kill me in a minute if you don't!' The creature was scrutinising Howard with its dozy eyes. There was something different about this boy and it seemed to know it. After a moment it decided it wasn't a good enough reason not to eat him, licking the lips of its many mouths and waggling some of its fingers in preparation for filleting.

'"*Shake out, break out, come over here let's make out,*"' Hubcap's voice was breaking, he couldn't even begin to remember the tune.

'Louder!' Howard shouted. 'Quickly!'

Hubcap bit his lip and closed his eyes, humming the song in his head. 'I hate my life,' he muttered again. '"*Maybe, baby, you could feel me with you.*"' His voice was growing louder as he got into the rhythm of it and the notes fell into place. '"*I know, by now, what every honey shouts out.*'" Now he really started to perform, swaying as he sang. "'*Cos baby let me hear you, I love it when I'm near you.*"' The creature had paused, something in its memory triggered by the song, Howard dangling above its snapping mouths as the main head tilted to one side and stared at Hubcap. The boy had begin to dance remembering the moves he'd seen the girls make to the song, all stood in line. Fist to the heart, hand to the head, kick your leg then sway back... '"*You're what I need, you make me shake, make me shake, make me shake out!*"' Hubcap did a little spin, then remembered where he was and looked around with some embarrassment.

'Adrian?' Howard said, looking straight into the creature's eyes. 'Adrian?'

It looked at him, a spark of something appearing for the first time.

'Adrian!' Howard shouted, watching the creature flinch slightly. 'There's a question we ask, Adrian. Do you know it? Where were *you*, Adrian? When it happened? Where *were* you?'

Chapter Twenty-Six

'... ADRIAN!' CAROLINE CALLED.

He did his best to ignore her and carried on scrubbing his hands beneath the tap.

'Adrian!'

There was that usual, *awful*, sound to her voice, as if the words were about to break up into laughter at any moment, laughter at *him*. What was it going to be now? He knew she wasn't on her own, he'd heard some other girls cackling when he'd been in the garage. Her horrid music—happy, jangly crap, like glitter for the ears—had filtered through the floorboards, spoiling his own tunes from the car stereo. He'd turned up MCR to drown it out.

'Adrian you're such a mong!' Her friend laughed at that. 'Come here! I know you can hear me.'

'Washing my hands.'

'*Oshing me ma,*' she mimicked as if he had uttered noises not words. 'Come here!'

He sighed, flicked the excess water off his hands and walked through to the lounge. *That* CD was playing

Shake Out by those Fadz arseholes. Caroline was *always* playing it.

'What?' he asked. 'I'm busy.'

'Messing about with that junk of scrap you call a car isn't being busy, Adrian. You know mum left me in charge.'

'Didn't.'

Caroline rolled her eyes. 'She *so* did, she knows you'd be dead within a day if left to fend for yourself, let alone a week.'

'Piss off.'

He turned to leave, but that bitch from year eleven, Sophie Horton, was stood in his way and he didn't want to push past her, the idea of touching her scared him.

'Adrian.' Caroline wanted something. The tone of her voice had changed as she realised she wouldn't get it if she pushed him too far. 'Look, let's not argue about it. It's stupid, I just wanted your help with something.'

'What?' he mumbled. It was better just to do it and then he could go. He hated being in his sister's presence when she was on her own, it was even worse when she had friends round, *especially* Sophie Horton. Besides, if he had to listen to this music for a minute longer. "Shake out, break out"? What did it even mean?

'Could you fetch Mum's CDs from the top shelf, I can't reach.'

Adrian couldn't believe her. 'Is that it? You were shouting for me just because of that?'

'Yeah, *lanky*, I can't reach them and you can.'

Adrian sighed, turned to the shelves and stretched up to the top shelf. 'Mum only put them up there so you couldn't get them.' He grabbed the handle of the leather folder the discs were kept in and suddenly felt his sister's nails scratch his belly as both she and Sophie yanked his tracksuit bottoms down. In shock, he dropped the folder which fell to the floor behind him. A few books that had been next to it went flying, one of which hit a china figurine on the mantelpiece, snapping it down the middle. Adrian fell back, losing his balance as his trousers caught him by the ankles. He landed on his back, naked from the waist down while the two girls laughed hysterically at him.

'I can't believe we set him up just to see that!' Sophie laughed, pointing at his groin. 'There's hardly anything there!'

Adrian was mortified, yanking at the elasticated waistband, desperate to cover himself up. That stupid song was still being all stupid and happy. It sounded like it was laughing at him. As for his sister, she wouldn't stop giggling even when he started screaming at her. In fact that just made her laugh more. Red-faced, he got his trousers back up, grabbed at her hair, and swung her at the wall with all his strength. She stopped laughing then, clawing at him with her nails, but he just roared and punched her hard on the chin. He heard one of her teeth snap as her jaw smacked together and she fell back.

Sophie was running. She had obviously decided to not hang about and fight him. Yeah. Not so pathetic *now* was he? Not so funny either. He caught up with her just before she could get the front door open, lashing out with his long arms and smacking her head into the frame. There was a cracking noise, and when she fell back there was blood pouring from beneath her fringe.

That was enough to snap him out of it. He knew he should never have touched her. What was he going to do now? What was he going to *do*?

He heard movement from the lounge. His sister. There was no way Caroline wouldn't make this work out as badly as possible for him. He was going to prison for this, or locked up in one of those places where they cut bits of your brain out, she'd see to that. She had always said he should be in one of those places, wearing those jackets that tied up your arms, taking the pills that made you go quieter and quieter.

He didn't want to be locked up, that was the simple truth of it. *He didn't want to be locked up*. That's the thought he held onto as he walked back into the lounge, picked up the heavy iron poker that sat in the coal scuttle by the fire and beat his sister to death with it. Once he was sure she wasn't going to move again, he took the poker to the front door and did the same to Sophie Horton. He was pretty sure he'd killed her already, but it didn't hurt to be certain.

He sat down on the stairs and thought for a while. His mum wouldn't be home until tomorrow. That was a whole day in which to clean up, get rid of the bodies and come up with an excuse. A whole day to build a perfect plan. Adrian could build anything, everyone said so. They knew he was no good at book stuff, words and numbers, but if you gave him something to build or fix, he could do that without even really thinking about it. Oil on his fingers and an engine opened up in front of him. Yes... it was the one thing guaranteed to make him relax.

He stood up, stepped over Sophie's body, walked into the kitchen and out through the internal door to the garage. The car was nothing special, an old Volkswagen Polo he'd bought it for next to nothing. Just scrap really, but he'd cleaned it up, replaced parts, got the engine working again. Then he'd begun improving things, tinkering, adding. 'Polishing a turd' his mum called it but then she had no interest in his mechanics, never had.

He dropped onto the wheeled trolley and slid under the car, happy just to lie there and smell the cement dust and oil. "*Make me shake...*" he sung to himself as he lay there remembering how it had felt to swing the poker again and again. He smiled.

At some point it got dark. He hadn't noticed, lost in his own thoughts. His stomach rumbled and he slid out from underneath the car and went into the kitchen. Looking in the fridge there was nothing to eat. Nothing he fancied anyway. '"*Make me shake out...*"' he muttered to himself.

There was a smell coming from the hallway, it had a metallic taste to it. He couldn't think what it was.

He drank some milk then wiped his furry top lip. He was suddenly feeling very tired. He walked into the hallway, flicking away the flies that seemed to linger by the front door. He wondered where his sister was, he hadn't seen her for hours. As much as she annoyed him he found himself wanting to spend a little time with her. He found her in the lounge, sleeping. He didn't want to wake her so he just lay down next to her, put his arm around her waist and slept for awhile.

A few hours later he was woken by a fly buzzing around his face. He swatted at it, peeled his face off his sister's cheek (embarrassing... he must have dribbled while he slept) and stood up. His back ached from where he had slept on the floor. The sun was coming up through the lounge window; it had that deep, egg yolk orange that only winter suns have. He walked out of the lounge and into the hall, deciding for some reason that it would be nice to see the sun rise. He had to fight to get the front door open, it seemed really stiff.

He took several deep lungfuls of the cold, morning air, coughing slightly as it burned its way along his throat. There were quite a few people in the street, certainly more than usual for that time of the day. Some of them were staring at him and he wondered if he had snot hanging out of his nose or something. He was just checking when he heard a loud ripping noise. It reminded him of the time under the car when he had caught his jeans in the exhaust casing and had to tear himself free. He looked up as something appeared in the sky above his head.

'Big,' he whispered as something popped inside his brain. A trickle of blood ran from his nose. All around him people had keeled over, falling dead to the floor. He ignored them.

He went back inside, feeling different somehow. His hunger had certainly returned and when he saw all the tasty meat that was lying just inside the door he could scarcely believe his luck. He sat down to eat his fill.

When his belly was satisfied he stood up to leave. A thought occurred to him.

'That's a really excellent pair of calf muscles,' he said, though there was nobody to hear him. 'Extremely well-developed.' They were certainly much better than his own, spindly legs. So many people just left things lying around that were so valuable. He told this to anyone that would listen, particularly when it got to the subject of his car. A lot of the parts he had used had been trashed before he found them, discarded... abandoned. He looked longingly at those calf muscles. Just wouldn't be right if he did the same would it? He began to strip them from the bone.

Later, with the new muscles in place he marched up and down the hall enjoying the extra spring they gave him.

'Great improvement,' he said and went into the lounge to see what he could salvage in there.

It got addictive, this modification. Over the next few weeks, he shopped for parts in the streets near his home, taking arms and legs, muscles and extra ligaments (to increase his response time).

One day he stood looking at his car, feeling what he could only describe as envy. If he could do it with the body parts then why not with this? He would never be perfect until he had the cylinders of a well-constructed engine pumping in his chest, heavy-gauge rubber for his soles, the thick, richness of a little unleaded in his veins. He fetched his tools and begun to work.

The creature that smashed its way through the outside wall of Adrian's house and into the quiet suburban street some weeks later was a sight to behold. The product of someone unable to stop adding, improving, modifying. It was considerably more than the sum of its parts but it had certainly lost something in the process. It had lost the one thing it needed to in order to truly become the monster it now was, it had lost...

Chapter Twenty-Seven

'...APTER T'

The creature dropped Howard with a howl and clutched at its deformed head.

Howard rolled along its distended belly, the wide mouths snapping at him as he passed. He bumped off the large piston in its thigh and landed on the ground in front of Hubcap.

'It's doing that because of my singing?' Hubcap shouted, the wails of the creature getting louder and louder.

'Kind of,' Howard replied, his hands over his ears.

'Cheeky git,' Hubcap said, pointing at the creature. 'I've got soul, pal!'

The creature was writhing, its skin rippling, arms flailing. Inside it, a young man called Adrian was fighting to get out, get all this horrible stuff off him so he could just *breathe*...

It began to unmake itself with the same speed and skill it had shown on its meals in the past. Its many fingers split the joins and wounds where it had added both metal and flesh, breaking itself down piece by piece. It flung muscles and valves, limbs and organs, desperate to get down to whatever was left in the middle. But when you get right down to it—and it did—what are all of us except spare parts?

Soon there was nothing left but piles of offal and machinery steaming in the dwindling light of the bonfire.

Chapter Twenty-Eight

'... WHICH IS WHEN I sang it to death.' Hubcap said with a wink.

'Doesn't surprise me.' Snakebite replied.

'What?' Hubcap gritted his teeth, it was so unfair. A whole camp of people and the only person he could find to talk to was this miserable git.

'The rubbish you young ' uns listen to.'

Hubcap felt—not for the first time—that the conversation was veering off into strange territory. 'What are you *talking* about?''Enough to kill anyone isn't it? All them pops and whistles...'

Hubcap shook his head. 'I don't listen to it, it's ages old. You're missing the point... the song reminded the person *inside* what it had been like before.'

'Horrible...'

'Eh?'

'Horrible song I bet. No, not even a song. More like...' Snakebite started to make sounds like a police car, waving his arms around in imitation of someone dancing at a club.

'No it was...' Hubcap desperately tried to think of the words that would make Snakebite understand. 'We just needed to remind him of the person he was before...'

Snakebite was still mimicking club dancing, waving his arms, eyes bulging.

Hubcap sighed and looked over to where Howard was stood chatting to Tank and Tiger. 'Can we go *now* please?' he shouted, 'and never *ever* come back?'

Howard smiled at Hubcap, he was suffering a bit himself.

'Just don't get him killed,' said Tank for about the hundredth time.

Howard put his best sincere face on. 'Well obviously, I'll try...'

'He's mouthy but vulnerable.' Tiger said.

Tank stared at him. 'I don't even know what that means.'

'Just look after him,' Tiger sighed.

'I will but, you know he's his own...'

'I can hardly bear this!' Tiger wailed, tears in his eyes.

Tank shook his head despairingly. 'You are so like my bloody mother right now... pull yourself together lad.' He turned back to Howard. 'Just don't get him killed.'

Chapter Twenty-Nine

LATER, STOOD IN his room, Hubcap stared at the drawings on his walls.

'I can't wait to get that crap painted over.'

Hubcap turned around to see Little Chef stood in the doorway. 'Don't you dare!' he replied with a smile. 'I want this place kept as a shrine!'

Little Chef shook his head. 'Shrines are for dead people.'

Hubcap shrugged. 'Give it time.'

'I don't think so. You're one of the most alive people I've ever met and I don't see that changing any time soon.' He looked out of the window at where the remains of the creature were being burned or wrapped in bags. 'That ugly thing certainly didn't manage it.'

'It killed enough other people.'

'Yes. Yes it did.' Little Chef patted the small of Hubcap's back. 'But not you. People die. A lot of them these days. The only way to deal with that is to work hard at *living*.'

He looked up at Hubcap and smiled. 'So sod off out of here and get on with it!'

Chapter Thirty

THEY WERE ON the road after lunch, packs on their back loaded with food and other supplies.

'You know which way we're going then?' asked Howard.

'Tank went on about it enough,' Hubcap grinned, tapping his head, 'it's etched in here as strongly as my own name.'

'Which is?'

'Hubcap.'

'But really?'

'Hubcap.'

'But actually?'

'Hubcap.'

'But your last name is?'

'Hubcap.'

'Except on your birth certificate where it says...?'

'Howard.'

'Really?'

'No, I would have killed myself long before now if it did.'

'Can I call you Speed Bump?'

'If you like being blind in one eye.' Hubcap stabbed the air with his middle finger.

'Traffic Cone?'

'I will shove the next one we see right up you.'

There was the fluttering of wings. Howard and Hubcap didn't notice as they were enjoying themselves too much.

'Exhaust Pipe?'

'Seriously—*Howie*—don't think I won't kill you because I will.'

'Glove Box?'

There was a loud cooing noise from behind them. They stopped walking, slowly looking over their shoulders. The cars were thick with pigeons, all staring at them.

'Hang on...' Hubcap reached for his pack.

'You've got the...?' Howard asked

'Yep.'

'Whirly noisy thing?'

'Yep.'

The pigeons ruffled their feathers.

Hubcap sighed. 'Except...'

'You forgot to pack it?'

'Yep.'

'Oh.'

Hubcap swung the pack back over his shoulder, moving slowly so as not to antagonise the birds.

'First rule of the Highway Code is "Don't Feed the Pigeons", right?' asked Howard.

'To be honest it's the second...'

'Oh yeah, so what's the first?'

'Run!'

And so they did.